GW00726702

Fee ɔ
Frenzy

A Salt Mine Novel

Joseph Browning   Suzi Yee

Text Copyright © 2019 by Joseph Browning and Suzi Yee

Published by Expeditious Retreat Press
Cover by J Caleb Design
Edited by Elizabeth VanZwolle

For information regarding Joseph Browning and Suzi Yee's novels and to subscribe to their mailing list, see their website at https://www.joseph-browning.com

To follow them on Twitter: https://twitter.com/Joseph_Browning

To follow Joseph on Facebook: https://www.facebook.com/joseph.browning.52

To follow Suzi on Facebook: https://www.facebook.com/SuziYeeAuthor/

To follow them on MeWee: https://mewe.com/i/josephbrowning

By Joseph Browning and Suzi Yee

THE SALT MINE NOVELS
Money Hungry
Feeding Frenzy
Ground Rules
Mirror Mirror
Bottom Line
Whip Smart
Rest Assured

Chapter One

"Mommy, Daddy—look at the lion!" The precocious five-year-old ran straight-legged toward the towering twenty-seven-foot-tall bronze statue that graced the entrance of the San Diego Zoo. She planted her small hands on the ground before kicking her legs up and roaring loudly. Her light-up sneakers flashed as her feet landed back on the pavement, and she fastidiously smoothed down her powder blue tulle tutu.

Her parents quickened their pace to catch up with their rambunctious daughter. This outing was her reward for her recent spate of good behavior at preschool. Mark would have been fine with buying her a toy, but Ella insisted on a family outing—something to build memories and encourage interaction and experience over material possessions. Did Olivia really need another toy or gadget?

"That's Rex." Ella knelt down and took her daughter's hand in hers. "He was one of the first animals at the zoo when it opened over 100 years ago!"

"Is Wrex still here? Can we see him?" Olivia asked curiously.

"No, sweetie. A hundred years is a long time for a lion to live," Mark answered, and patted her on the back. They had recently had a long talk about death when her goldfish was ceremoniously flushed down the toilet.

Olivia's brow furrowed. "So he's dead?"

"Yes, but they took good care of him while he was living here," Ella replied.

After a quiet moment, her high-pitched voice inquired incredulously, "Was he really that big?"

"No, but he was so mighty they had to make the statue that big for people to recognize him," Mark responded.

Olivia considered this for a while and then slipped her other hand into her dad's large one, nodding in acceptance at his explanation.

They approached the gate, syncing their steps so Olivia could swing between them. His plan was to arrive at open, grab a close parking space, and beat the rush—the season of zoo babies was just starting, and the less organized families would roll up sometime around eleven or maybe two or three, if this was their second stop of the day. Sadly, the best-made plans often went awry when you have a five-year-old. They shuffled into line—short in comparison to the queue for ticket-purchasing patrons.

Mark pulled out their annual passes as Ella reviewed the rules with Olivia—no running away, always stay next to mommy or daddy, no sweets or drinks since they brought their own snacks, and she only gets one souvenir, so choose wisely. She solemnly nodded her brown curly mop in agreement. He let his eyes wander as they waited in line and saw one child not much younger than Olivia on one of those retractable leashes, and wished that his wife wasn't so adamantly against them—it would make taking Olivia out less harrowing, given her tendency to bolt whenever she was excited.

He gave Ella a knowing glance as their child prattled off animal facts she had learned at school before nodding in acknowledgement at the wisdom his five-year-old was imparting as they made their way into the zoo. Ella replied with a sardonic gleam in her eyes, hidden in a kind smile— *you'll thank me when she's too embarrassed to even be seen with you in ten years.* Mark knew she was right, but that didn't mean he had to admit it.

They passed the gate and Ella took Olivia straight to the restrooms. Mark checked his phone as he waited for them to come back. After a few minutes, Olivia came barreling out so quickly she pounced on him before he managed to put his phone away. "I got you, Daddy!"

He slid his phone into his pocket and feigned surrender with his other hand. "You caught me!" he conceded, skillfully preventing this from turning into a game of tag in the large thoroughfare.

Ella approached them, grinning at the pair. "What do you want to see first, pumpkin?"

"I want to see the lelaphants!" she exclaimed, but dutifully kept her position between her parents. She slipped her hands into theirs and waited for them to lead the way.

The inquisitive child paused at each viewing area along the way, and when coupled with stops at photo-op sites, what was listed as a twenty-minute walk on the colorful zoo map became an hour excursion on the sunny spring day. As they rounded the corner into Elephant Odyssey, the gray concrete sidewalks turned into beige sandstone pavers while the walls and pillars were camouflaged in light brown with faint traces of russet. There was a zoo educator at the pronghorns next to the camels—apparently it was feeding time.

"Olivia, do you want to see them feed the animals?!" Ella used her enthusiastic mom voice. Olivia vigorously nodded her head and pulled her parents in that direction. As they approached, the zoo educator's amplified voice carried over the crowd comprised mostly of younger children and their minders.

"The zoo is home to five pronghorn bucks—that's right, we have all boys here. They are native to western North American in the open prairies and deserts. In the wild, they travel in herds for safety. When a predator finds them, they can run away really fast—the only land animal that is faster than them are cheetahs!" The mention of the large predatory cat brought oohs and ahhs of appreciation.

"They are ungulates, which means they have hooves—just

like deer and antelopes—but they are special because they grow horns, not antlers." The educator looked over her shoulder and pointed at one of the bucks behind her. "See his horns? They come to one point, unlike antlers that spread out in all directions. Pronghorns are the only animals with forked horns that shed every year. These fellas just finished growing their new horns for this year, but they'll lose them in late autumn and grow a brand new pair next year."

Another figure emerged within the enclosure through a door in the back. He waved at the zoo educator and her audience before wheeling in a load of feed and closing the door behind him. "It's just about lunch time for the pronghorns. Pronghorns are herbivores. Who can tell me what an herbivore eats?" A chorus of childish voices yelled out answers.

"Grass!"

"Plants!"

"Herbs!"

"That's right!" the zoo educator replied. "Herbivores only eat plants. Here at the zoo, we feed our pronghorns alfalfa pellets, hay, and fresh vegetables—"

Her presentation was abruptly halted by a shrill cry coming from the enclosure as the largest of the bucks charged, piercing the food deliverer in the gut. Screaming in pain, the zookeeper managed to maneuver the wheelbarrow between himself and the buck that was backing up for another charge, only to be gored on his flanks by two of the other pronghorns. Stunned by the attack, he looked toward the exit, hoping for a clear path out of the enclosure, but the final pair of bucks was advancing toward him from that direction. Finding retreat impossible, the zookeeper yelled as loudly as he could to frighten the animals and withdrew into a stony corner, dragging his wheelbarrow and using it as a shield of sorts. As the pronghorn repeatedly charged, crimson seeped through his clothing and he repeatedly yelled for help over the clatter of horn on metal.

Olivia loosed a shriek at the sight of blood as Mark scooped her up and took off running. She buried her face in his chest, and her tears soaked into his shirt. The crowd's screams broke the educator's shock as she directed all the guests away from the exhibit. She grabbed the radio attached to her shoulder and called over the secure channel, "Animal attack in Elephant Odyssey in the pronghorn enclosure! Repeat: animal attack in Elephant Odyssey in the pronghorn enclosure. Animals are still contained, but we have an injured zookeeper trapped inside with the animals. Requesting immediate response team!"

Chapter Two

Detroit, Michigan, USA
1st of April, 6:00 a.m. (GMT-4)

The patter of soft rain on broad banana leaves roused Teresa Martinez from her slumber. She fumbled for her phone and swiped the first snooze as she burrowed deeper under her comforter. She stretched lazily on her cherry wood sleigh bed that had finally arrived from the West Coast last week. The weeks-long wait that had started with a marathon packing session in Portland had finally come to an end. She'd decadently watched the movers load most of her worldly possessions onto a truck in Oregon, only to unload in Michigan. Martinez had briefly contemplated moving herself, but then vowed that she was too old and made too much money to do that again—she had reached the time in her life where her furniture was actually nice enough to move instead of replace, and that stuff was heavy. Ruefully, Martinez had to admit she missed the simplicity of cramming everything she owned into a U-Haul and plotting her way across the country—not enough to actually do it, of course, but enough to get nostalgic about it.

She spent all weekend unpacking, doing laundry, and setting

up her new home…well, her temporary new home. As soon as her place in Portland was sold—the realtor assured her it was a seller's market—she could start looking for places to buy and fix up in Michigan in earnest. In the meantime, Wilson's rental house was a welcome change from hotel life, and it checked all the boxes—it was close to work, it already had a basement set up for conducting magic, and it was reasonably priced—no doubt because of the three ghosts that shared the house with her.

Martinez was dubious at first. Not just because of the spirits, but the prospect of mixing personal life with work gave her pause. Was having a colleague as your landlord really a good idea, especially if you were both supernatural agents for a black ops organization? However, as there was nothing in the employee handbook prohibiting it and Wilson hardly struck her as the Mr. Roper type, she went ahead and made the call.

A majestic bird crooned from her phone—had it been five minutes already? She rolled around on her thousand thread count Egyptian cotton sheets that faintly smelled of lavender before rubbing the sleep from her eyes and turning off the alarm for good. A twinge rippled through her lower back as she rose from bed; she muttered about too many hours hunched over boxes as she made her way to the ibuprofen in the medicine cabinet in the bathroom. The smell of fresh-brewed coffee wafted from the kitchen; thankfully, she'd remembered to program the coffee maker before she went to bed last night.

It was still dark out as Martinez readied for work, fastening the errant strands of hair before trading in her flannel pajamas for her work attire: her favorite dark gray suit that she had left in Portland and subsequently hadn't worn in months. It was little snugger that she remembered, but the crisp starched lines still held as she appraised herself in the mirror. Now that she had her kitchen again, she could return to her routine—no more meals from takeout boxes and paper bags. She slung on her shoulder holster before tucking away her Glock 43 and extra magazines.

She dressed her coffee and reverently took her first sip before screwing on the lid of the travel mug. Breakfast and packed lunch safely stowed into her leather bag, she slid on her flat boots with traction for the late winter slush; it was one of her biggest pet peeves about female law enforcement on TV and in movies—no one in their right mind chooses to chase down a perp in stiletto heels, along with a blowout and full makeup, of course.

Martinez patted herself down to make sure she had everything: keys, wallet, phone, ID badge, gun, bag, and coffee. Keys in hand, she called out to Millie, Wolfhard, and the silent member of the ethereal trio, giving them her typical farewell, "Feel free to haunt the hell out of any burglars or intruders while I'm away," before closing and locking the front door.

Her pitch-black Dodge Charger SRT Hellcat purred in the driveway, and Martinez briefly checked her phone while the engine and her leather seat warmed up. She surfed through the overabundance of fake headlines designed for April Fools, chuckling at the announcement that the Westminster Dog Show will officially include the giant miniature poodle in the list of recognized breeds. She turned on her satellite radio to the real news before shifting the car into reverse and flipping on her headlights. A polar vortex had wreaked havoc on North America once again, covering Michigan in blankets of snow and bitter cold. Between her visit to Portland and training at Camp Perry, she had missed the worst of it, and spring was edging its way forward. Still, Martinez felt a little like Charlie Brown with the football—she dared not hope for good weather.

She steered her new car toward the highway and took in as much bad news as she could before switching to something more upbeat and energetic on her way to Zug Island. As far as regular employees on the island were concerned, she was Tessa Marvel, Assistant Director of Acquisitions at Discretion Minerals, a company that had been mining the vast salt deposits on the isolated island for over a hundred years. Martinez understood the need for a cover alias, but it stretched even her imagination that salt mining was such a booming business, it required not only a Director of Acquisitions, but that the director needed an assistant as well.

Unbeknownst to the general public, the CIA had owned and operated Discretion Minerals for over six decades. Carved in its depths—metaphorically and literally—was the Salt Mine, a black ops agency that monitored and managed supernatural activity. Unofficially, the Salt Mine was funded by both the FBI and the CIA, although it was never a cited line item on even the black budgets' books. Technically, the Salt Mine didn't exist, because everyone knows that magic and the supernatural didn't exist. Except it did, and it rarely played nice.

If someone had told her six months ago that she was going to move to Detroit to become one of seven agents tasked with investigating and containing magical threats, she would have laughed her ass off. Yet, here she was, almost four months into her new job. Within the first six weeks, she had met a devil, broke into a former crime scene to perform magical reconnaissance, survived an attack by a demon-possessed Brit, and recovered a mythical artifact.

Martinez pulled into the security checkpoint and held out her ID badge. After a short burst of friendly banter with George, the Monday morning guard, Agent Martinez pulled into a parking spot and, with a quick flip of a titanium key, caught the elevator down into the Salt Mine. "Good morning, Ms. Martinez," Angela Abrams's chipper voice carried over the tinny intercom. Martinez plopped her bag and weapon into the slot that emerged within the wall for scanning.

"Good morning, Abrams. Have a good weekend?" she politely inquired before sipping her coffee.

"Oh, you know, the usual…although I could use a second for a double date next weekend," Abrams hinted none-too-subtly. The attendant let a small smile slip from her side of the translucent ballistic glass.

Martinez managed to swallow her coffee instead of spit it out. "Thanks for thinking of me, but I have to pass. I have a lot of unpacking to do, and my office could use some work."

"Your loss—Harry's cousin is super cute," her perky tone clipped coquettishly. Abrams's mood had vastly improved over the past couple of weeks, and for that, Martinez was eternally grateful to Harry, whoever he may be. A metallic buzz sounded, and the door opened. "Have a nice day, and let me know if you change your mind."

"Will do," Martinez answered with a perfunctory smile. She holstered her weapon on the other side and picked up her bag, briskly making her way down to the next bank of elevators. Once inside, she pressed her eye and palm to their respective scanners and pushed the button for the fifth floor. The metal box descended further into the Salt Mine.

As Martinez made her way to her office, she passed dusty doors bearing names of agents past, imaging how different it would be if all the offices were filled with operatives instead of just seven. When she reached the door labeled "Lancer," she held her palm against the scanner until she heard the click of the lock disengage. She turned the handle and nudged the door open with her hip while she reached for the light switch on the wall. Soft white light flooded the room from the circular brass fixture in the center of the ceiling, a blessed change from the cold-war chic fluorescent lights that came with the office.

Rather than fight the mid-century vibe of the office she'd inherited, Martinez decided to lean into it. She cherry-picked the best of the functional items that were already there, and supplemented them with pieces to update the workspace to the twenty-first century. She kept one of the steel filing cabinets, but traded in the sterile built-in shelving for metal and glass cabinets in a dusky blue-gray. She gladly removed the ratty plaid couch in the corner and replaced it with two lounge chairs and the matching ottomans that tucked under the seats. When coupled with a floor lamp between them and a pair of circular coffee tables—one slightly smaller and shorter than the other for easy collapsible storage—the nook was downright cozy. If she were still in Portland, she would have combed the antique stores and flea markets for finds, but in the face of Michigan winter and having to move everything herself, she opted for IKEA instead. Martinez was always a sucker for things you could assemble with just an Allen wrench and your wits.

She deposited her coffee and bag on her desk before hanging her jacket on the chrome rack. She'd swapped the boxy desk for an adjustable workspace, complete with an ergonomic office chair, stool, and anti-fatigue mat to accommodate a range of postures. Two repurposed nightstands stood on either side of her seat, providing storage space that left the top clear of clutter. She started her computer and turned on her two wide monitors while she picked up the well-worn manila folder in her in-basket, OFFICIAL – SM EYES ONLY inked in black. Martinez was still in training, but Leader started sending her the dailies a few weeks ago to help acclimate her into the routine. Soon enough, Lancer would be expected to work independently, but thankfully, today wasn't that day.

Today, she had a date with Chloe and Dot, the conjoined twins collectively regarded as the librarians the custodians of the highly restricted sixth floor of the Mine. Their eidetic memories and expertise in all things supernatural made them ideal resources and tutors, and Martinez needed all the help she could get. The first couple of months were heavy on the didactic reading, just to get an adequate foundation. Now, she had to learn how to use magic.

At first, it seemed like paradoxical; if magic was—to paraphrase Dot—"just shit," why did Salt Mine agents use it? Like poison, the devil is in the details and dose. Sure, magic always came at a price, and the price was always greater than its benefit, but if one knew what the price was and how to mitigate the cost, theoretically a practitioner could wield it responsibly in the pursuit of containing malevolent, dangerous, or unfettered magic. Wilson had likened it to firearms—the world arguably would be a better place without them, but since they exist, law enforcement's use of them was necessary and safe as long as they understood how and when to wield them responsibly.

Magic items were easy; the power was imbued in the item

itself and she was simply using it, like turning on a flashlight—technically, she flipped the switch, but the power wasn't coming from her. It was simply a matter of knowing how they worked and how to use them safely. Martinez had experience in using magic items from her first few weeks, and had found a handful of worthy causes to which she donated time and money to defray the negative karmic cost. But it wasn't the same with practicing magic; you had to draw the energy to power the magic from an unconscious well within you. Casting spells, performing rituals, and summoning creatures required something personal to the practitioner, and each person was unique in their approach.

For weeks, Chloe and Dot poked around her subconscious with a proverbial dowsing rod, giving her minor cantrips to cast in trial and error until one day, Martinez successfully changed a white gerbera daisy's petals blue. Much to the agent's chagrin, they had found her unconscious well rooted in Catholicism. Not that Martinez was a devotee, and her last confession was so long ago, she wasn't even sure she counted as a lapsed Catholic at this point. Apparently, however, twelve years at a Catholic girls' school left its mark deep in her subconscious and that was where her magic would be powered, as long as she didn't try to understand it with her conscious mind. Martinez laughed at that—no worries there.

With that mystery solved, the twins tailored Martinez's study, assigning her exercises to access and control her power as well as compiling lists of spells and resources most amenable to such energy. Martinez could imagine how difficult and scary this process might be for native magicians without the benefit of esoteric tutors. It would be so easy for magically inclined individuals who stumbled into this ability to misuse their powers or get themselves into some serious trouble. Without anyone to tell them the rules and navigate the pitfalls, they were left to intuit everything on their own, or take the word of supernatural creatures—many of which were untrustworthy, to say the least.

Martinez drank her breakfast—a protein shake—and continued her reading for another hour before a buzz broke her concentration. A red light blinked on the box affixed to the corner of her desk. "Martinez here," she spoke after depressing the button.

David LaSalle's pleasant tenor tumbled out of the speaker, "Leader requests your presence at her office on the fourth floor at nine o'clock. Chloe and Dot have been notified of the change in plans."

Martinez raised an eyebrow. Leader was Salt Mine's commander-in-chief, and while Martinez saw her in passing, she was rarely beckoned to her office. Leader remained a terrifyingly enigmatic figure, and the occasional five seconds she took to swipe her palm and eye on the elevator's scanner to grant Martinez access to the sixth floor for training with Chloe and Dot did little to break the facade. Martinez looked up at the wall clock and noted the time. "Okay, see you then."

Chapter Three

Detroit, Michigan, USA
1ˢᵗ of April, 7:45 a.m. (GMT-4)

"Good morning, Mr. Wilson. Late night?" Abrams playfully teased the unusually tardy agent.

"Just wrapping up a case that went long," Wilson tersely replied, betraying his agitation as he deposited his briefcase and firearm clumsily into the metal slot and smoothed back his hair. He hated being late. Not only did it transform his otherwise ten-minute commute into a half-hour in gridlock, it was a moral affront. He couldn't remember the last time he overslept. If he wasn't absolutely certain that his home at the 500 was an impenetrable fortress, he would have thought someone had set all his clocks forward as an April Fools' joke.

"Have a good day." Abrams smiled from the other side of the ballistic glass and buzzed him through once the scan was complete. Wilson discerned a tone of amusement in her salutation. He regained his composure and gave a curt nod as he passed through the threshold and collected his belongings. He slipped his Glock 26 into his holster and gripped his attaché, picking up his pace to the next bank of elevators.

Wilson blamed Aloysius, the flamboyant owner and operator of 18 is 9, Detroit's premier goth dance club tucked away in the warehouse district. Were it not for his call, Wilson would have spent his Sunday evening in relative peace and quiet. Instead, he'd spent the better part of the night under black lights scanning for a magic user new to the scene. Aloysius—himself a practitioner of the arts who had a misspent youth—knew the smell of trouble, and Wilson was loathe to admit the club owner had pretty good instincts for that sort of thing. Plus, one of Aloysius's tips paid off in the recovery of a smuggled cultural artifact of supernatural importance, and Wilson liked to keep his informants relatively happy.

Wilson had known better than to arrive any earlier than 10:00 p.m.; even on a Sunday night, the dance floor was far from empty. Once he zeroed in on his prey, a young man in his late teens to early twenties dressed in all black pleather with an embroidered burgundy cloak, Wilson wasted no time—after all, this was a friendly visit to caution and collect information. The fledgling magician had balls; the little shit tried to ensorcell him without any success when Wilson made his approach. Agents of the Salt Mine had training to resist such measures, especially such amateurish attempts. Aloysius had looked overly pleased when Wilson escorted the young man to a back room made available for a private conversation. It made Wilson wonder what faux pas the poor sap had committed against the sweaty, bald club owner—had he insulted his signature yellow-green-purple ensemble, or perhaps out-charmed one of Aloysius's quarries?

Wilson slowed his pace as he neared his office, presenting his palm to the door scanner. Once inside, he fired up his computer and finished his coffee while it booted. A quick skim of the dailies revealed nothing interesting or out of the ordinary, and the agent pulled up his keyboard and monitor. He methodically entered the new magician into the Salt Mine database: name, address, date of birth, picture, fingerprints, and magical signature.

He opened the file on the fragment of Mayan codex he'd recently recovered from private ownership. The remaining piece of the fragile folded book made of bark was exquisitely preserved given its age, and would have remained stashed away in someone's personal collection had it not contained instructions on how to summon Chaac. Safely tucked away and catalogued somewhere on the sixth floor of the Salt Mine, all that remained was the paperwork. Wilson dove into his work, and the rapid staccato of his keyboard drummed out his account.

The olive box on his desk broke his focus with its flashing light and intermittent buzzing. "This is Wilson," he answered as he pushed the button.

"Leader requests your presence at her office on the fourth floor at nine o'clock," the familiar voice of Leader's secretary-cum-bodyguard sounded.

Wilson consulted his Girard-Perregaux watch. "I'll be there in thirty minutes," he replied before breaking the connection and resuming his typing.

Wilson was surprised to find Martinez waiting for the elevator. Were he not afraid of being late, he would have stayed back and waited for the next one.

"Good morning, Wilson," Martinez called over her shoulder. It was too late to retreat.

"Good morning, Martinez," he politely greeted her. "How is training going?"

"I survived Camp Perry and missed the last cold snap, so I can't complain," she replied nonchalantly. The elevator doors opened and Martinez provided the requisite eye and palm scans before pushing the button for level four as Wilson entered and moved to the side.

"Headed to Chloe and Dot?"

"That was the original plan, but I'm actually going to see Leader."

Wilson inquired, "Her nine o'clock?"

Martinez turned her head. "How did you know?"

Wilson drily replied, "It would appear we are both her nine o'clock."

The trim yet towering stature of David LaSalle greeted them at the elevator. He bid them to follow, steering them through the white sparkling hallways carved out of the salt. "Fulcrum and Lancer for your nine o'clock, ma'am," he announced.

The petite woman behind the desk raised her steely gray eyes from the open files in front of her. "Thank you, David," Leader responded before motioning the agents to take a seat. She waited for the door to shut completely before continuing. "Two days ago, a group of five pronghorns attacked a zookeeper at the San Diego Zoo. All five animals are in quarantine. The zookeeper is still alive after emergency surgery, but hasn't regained consciousness. This is the third occurrence of an animal attack at a zoo perpetrated by non-predatory, low-aggression species in the past three months. I would like the two of you to fly out today and investigate."

Wilson cleared his throat. "Anything in particular that flagged this incident as supernatural in nature?"

"Facial recognition picked up the same man as a zoo patron for three consecutive days preceding the attack. Our team of analysts went back and reviewed surveillance video near the other two zoos, and found he was at each location within a few days after their animal attacks." Leader picked up a stack of photos from the file and fanned them out on her desk, facing the agents. "See anyone you recognize?"

"Lukin," Wilson muttered under his breath with bile.

"Exactly," Leader replied as she leaned against the edge of her desk next to the photos and folded her arms.

"I'm sorry, but who is Lukin?" Martinez interjected.

Wilson's stare bore into the photos as he flipped through them again. "Alexander Petrovich Lukin, Sasha to his friends.

He's Ivory Tower."

"Ivory Tower—as in the old Soviet counterpart to the Salt Mine?" Martinez queried curiously. "I thought they were largely declawed after the fall of the Soviet Union."

"They were never disbanded, merely shifted into the hands of the ruling oligarchy," Leader answered succinctly. "And if the Ivory Tower is interested in this, then so are we."

Wilson squared the pictures and his emotional equilibrium as he placed everything back into the file. "Wait, you said he was seen within days after the first two attacks, but he was at the San Diego Zoo before the attack? Is he looking for something or perpetrating it?"

Leader pivoted back to her side of the desk. "That's for the two of you to figure out. If Lukin is searching for something, I want you to find it first. If the Ivory Tower is responsible for this attack, I want you to get to the bottom of the hows and whys, and shut it down." Leader took a seat. "Discreetly, of course"

Martinez scoffed in her head; the last case she'd worked on with Wilson ended with burning down the country home of a demon-possessed lawyer, and Leader hardly batted an eye. Martinez hated to think what Leader considered non-discreet. "Not that I wouldn't love to spend this time of year in Southern California instead of Michigan, but why send me, especially if you know something supernatural is afoot? I'm still in training."

Leader shifted in her seat, unaccustomed to her methods

being questioned. "Trust me, it's better for you to meet the Ivory Tower with an experienced agent by your side. Plus, Lukin and Fulcrum have history, so you will be the face of the investigation. The longer the Ivory Tower is in the dark, the better."

"She's right," Wilson concurred. "At this point, the likelihood that anyone knows you're Salt Mine is slim to none; the same can't be said for any of the other agents. The previous animal attacks occurred on US soil, so if you go in as Special Agent Martinez of the FBI, it shouldn't raise any alarms."

"Unless you have any other questions, I recommend you go down and collect Martinez's field kit from Harold and get packing. Your flight leaves in four hours." Leader dismissed them with a wave of her hand.

LaSalle collected the pair of agents and flashed his palm and eye on the scanners before pressing floor six on the elevator panel. Martinez waited until the door closed before speaking. "I'll read the official files on the plane, but is there anything you would like me to know about the Ivory Tower, unofficially?"

They both stared straight ahead at the elevator door, and the electric hum of the lights and moving parts filled the silence. Wilson's face shifted as he alternately clinched and relaxed his jaw. "The biggest difference between the Salt Mine and the Ivory Tower is what they do with the magic once they have it. The Salt Mine buries it so no one can use it. The Ivory Tower is more permissive; the ends always justify the means, especially if it is funded by an oligarch. They regard it as practical efficiency. I call it foolish hubris."

"And Harold?"

"Harold Weber. He's our magical tech version of Q, and makes sure we have equipment tailored to our unique line of work. He works on the sixth floor with Chloe and Dot," Wilson replied stoically.

"So the briefcase and the bullets?"

"Both built off his original specs."

"Does this mean I get my own luggage this time?" Martinez joked.

"Good to see you are aiming high, Martinez," Wilson quipped back.

The doors opened to twinkling corridors carved out of the salt. They passed through the etched silver door and the vast aisles of books that had become routine to Martinez over the past few months. The agents approached the sprawling wooden counter and found the librarians behind a tower of tomes.

"Martinez?! We were told that you weren't coming to training today," Chloe chimed up, and nudged her sister to turn her attention away from the stacks. "Pleasure to see you as always, Wilson." He gave the more gregarious of the twins a nod. "What brings you two to the sixth floor?"

"We're here to see Weber," Wilson responded.

Dot snorted and picked up a receiver. "Earth to Harold—you have visitors." She returned the piece to its cradle before

Chloe spoke up.

"You really should be nicer to him. We have to work with him, you know."

"Chloe, you're doing something different with your hair. It really suits you," Martinez interceded before a full chastisement threatened to erupt.

The right side of the conjoined twins reflexively patted her hair. "How nice of you to notice!" Chloe cast her brown eyes sideways at Dot while her tone threw shade on Wilson in equal measure. "So I take it you're on a mission. Anything you can tell us?"

Martinez waffled, uncertain of protocol. Wilson stepped in, saying, "Martinez needs a quick primer on the Ivory Tower and Alexander Petrovich Lukin."

That garnered Dot's attention. "The only thing more disturbing than running into old friends is crossing paths with old enemies."

"How exciting! Reminds me of the good old days of cloak and dagger," Chloe cooed. Martinez's brow knitted in confusion—if she had to guess their age, the twins didn't look more than ten years older than her, and she was barely alive when the Berlin Wall fell. "We have aged well," Chloe added as an aside before addressing Wilson. "Tell me, is Sasha still as handsome as ever?" Dot rolled her eyes, and Chloe could sense the judgment emanating from her other half. "Just because he's an untrustworthy ass doesn't mean he's not easy on the eyes."

"Forgive her," Dot apologized. "She has a soft spot for the brooding type—equal parts angry and miserable, with just a dash of self-loathing."

Martinez shrugged. "To each their own. People would call that 'emo' now but that was never my thing. Fix it or get over it, but stop whining about it already." Wilson let a small approving smile surface on his usually impassive mien.

They heard Weber's approach well before they saw him, as the salt ground under his brisk shuffling gait. Martinez was not wholly prepared for the sight of the inventor as he turned the corner. His gray hair was mostly tamed, with an errant tuff sticking up from a pair of safety goggles hoisted on his head. His bright eyes belied a quick and curious mind behind the thick glasses. Still wearing his work apron with copious pockets, Weber nodded to the librarians and addressed the visitors in a crisp voice, "Agent Fulcrum." He nodded to Wilson, who returned the gesture. "And this must be Lancer?" Martinez automatically greeted the question with a smile and extended her hand, which the bespectacled man stared at before extracting his own from his pocket. "This way."

Wilson liked Weber—he was fastidious without being fussy, and you would never catch him dishing about who he found attractive. If it wasn't about a piece of equipment, Weber wasn't interested. Wilson and Martinez followed the gentleman to his workshop located at the end of a corridor branching off the main hall. Weber liked his quiet, and the twins liked not hearing or smelling when his inventions went awry.

Weber considered himself primarily an inventor that dabbled with magic in the pursuit of better field tools. His guiding principle was elegant efficiency. Whenever possible, he would get his hands on the latest piece of CIA tech and imbue it with a practical magical implication—he loathed unitaskers. He took inspiration from modern investigative techniques and spycraft, and took pleasure in weaving those principles into the supernatural agent's arsenal. What he did was important—using magic items bore less of a karmic cost than casting spells to the same effect, and more important to the agent, it emitted its own signature rather than the user's. It allowed agents to maneuver in esoteric anonymity, and knowing that his gadgets were saving lives in the field allowed him to abide the long hours and occasional setbacks.

Weber didn't waste time on niceties and dove right into the equipment, much of which was familiar to Martinez as it was a near duplicate of what Wilson had on their first mission together. Her suitcase was nearly identical to Wilson's, but it held more goodies on the inside.

"I took the liberty of including a few extra pieces, given the nature of the mission and your relatively new status with the Salt Mine," he explained as she ran her fingers over the three disparate items inside her luggage. He picked up a slim black cylinder that fit into the palm of his hand. "This appears to be your run-of-the-mill e-cigarette, but it is also an electronic disruptor that can also shut down WiFi in discrete areas. You point this end to whatever you want to jam, good to ten meters, and press this button—it toggles on and off. But that's not all it does." His wizened hands unscrewed the tube. "Look inside… what do you see?"

Martinez tilted the tube in the light. "Looks like sigils…is this a saltcaster?!"

A broad grin erupted on his face. "Very good, Lancer. You can load it ahead of time and it won't distribute the salt until these two notches are lined up and the button is depressed. And it goes without saying, do not inhale in that mode." He reassembled the e-cigarette before moving on to a necklace with an amber pendent. "This is a periapt that absorbs magic directed against the wearer. It won't help against supernatural creatures physically attacking you or effects in the general area, but if someone tries to charm you or track you, this should consume the magic. Note, it only works if you are wearing it." His words were directed at Martinez, but his line of sight was squarely directed at Wilson.

"Don't see a lot of guys wearing amber medallions these days, Weber," Wilson spoke in his defense.

The inventor mumbled something about pearls to swine under his breath before moving on. He picked up the rosary beads and placed them in Martinez's hands. "If you have to cast a spell, these will give you a little boost. They are hollow spheres made from a special alloy with runes cast on the inside of the large beads. Peace be with you."

"And also with you," Martinez instinctually answered.

"Ah, a lapsed Catholic..." Weber sighed. "Don't think I forgot about you, Fulcrum," he tutted as he opened one of his many drawers. "I've been tinkering with something I think you'll like." He pulled out a compass and let it dangle on its lead. "It's a magical tracker." Weber's baby blues twinkled as he opened up the back, which was covered with occult markings carefully etched into the metal. "If you take a sample of something affected by the magic in question and place it in here, the compass will follow the signature. You still have to identify the signature the old-fashioned way, but this allows you to track it if you are hot on its trail and it hasn't been scrubbed."

Wilson examined the compass and practiced opening and closing all the parts. "Weber, you're a real mensch."

The older man flipped his hand dismissively. "Don't get too excited; it only works to about a hundred meters and sometimes the needle gets a little jumpy if there is a ley line nearby, but it's a working prototype." He paused briefly, weighing his next words. "Do me a favor. If you get a chance to land a blow on the Ivory Tower, kick it in the balls for me."

"Will do," Wilson agreed as he pocketed the newest piece of his kit.

Chapter Four

Detroit, Michigan, USA
1st of April, 12:50 p.m. (GMT-4)

Martinez nimbly glided through the gray, chrome, and glass architecture of the Detroit Metro Airport before boarding her plane. Martinez and Wilson may have been assigned the case together, but good tactics required they work independently. She would publically investigate the animal attacks and gain entry to people and places with her badge; he would covertly investigate the supernatural aspects and any leads he could get on Lukin. It was agreed that they should travel separately, she as Special Agent Teresa Martinez of the FBI and he as Davis Watson, common man on vacation getting a dose of warm sunny Southern California.

Although they would be on the same flight and staying at the same hotel, their travel arrangements were booked independently. The flight was pretty full, but that didn't stop Wilson from upgrading to first class. Martinez resisted the urge to glare at him while she moved past him on her way to the economy seats, passing the flight attendant en route with his beverage of choice. At least she had a window seat.

She did a final check on her e-mail before plugging her phone into the USB power port and switching it to airplane mode. It was a five-hour flight and she had a lot of reading to do, starting with the animal attacks. The first attack was at Happy Farm Petting Zoo in Tempe, Arizona, a sole proprietorship owned and operated by Milo Perkins that made nearly six digits in a good year. Shortly after New Years, a small flock of sheep attacked a four-year-old girl visiting the zoo, biting at her hands, arms, and legs. Her parents asserted the petting zoo was at fault, while the owner insisted it was simply an unfortunate accident—a reflexive response to overzealous contact on the child's part. Martinez winced; even if the kid was a terror just one act away from inspiring an Oompa Loompa song, blaming the victim never comes off well.

Martinez shifted in her seat as a petite woman in her 50s took the middle seat next to her. They exchanged polite smiles as Martinez pulled out her earbuds and played some instrumental background music to discourage conversation. Returning to her phone, she flipped through the articles to glean the pertinent facts: all the sheep in the pen were ewes— no rams—and it wasn't mating season nor were any lambs present. One animal expert interviewed noted that sheep can get surly in the right circumstances and are certainly prone to herd mentality, but generally, a rams' horns or the strong kick of the back legs were the dangerous ends of sheep, not biting. At last report, the petting zoo was closed pending investigation from state public health agencies. The offending animals were put down and cleared of rabies by brain sampling and testing. Mr. Perkins declined further comment, attributing his silence to "unresolved litigation."

The captain's velvety voice came over the speaker; Martinez had become accustomed to the drill: flight information, weather conditions at destination, seats in upright positions, seat belts fastened while you are seated, please turn off and stow your large electronic devices for takeoff and place smaller electronic devices into airplane mode. The flight attendants took to the front of their sections with their safety accoutrements, and she paused her reading and readied the next set of files on her phone for once they reached altitude. Even though she didn't need to turn off her phone—thankfully the FAA had finally come to its senses about that—she preferred not to read during takeoff.

Martinez lifted the window shade as the engines powered up and the plane started moving. She always loved takeoff, watching the ground fall beneath them until the landscape looked like a miniature world below. The air and metal rattled as it gained speed, and Martinez felt a lightness in her chest and stomach as the plane ascended. She sat back, giving the woman next to her an oblique line of sight; soon the view turned into fluffy clouds dotting the bright midday sky. Eventually, the seatbelt light turned off and the captain addressed the cabin, giving everyone permission to turn on all portable electronic devices, even larger laptops, as long as they were in airplane mode. Martinez popped her ears a few times and dove into the second animal attack.

It occurred at Hillcrest Park Zoo, a small but reputable zoo in New Mexico. Operated by the city of Clovis, it was a part of the larger Hillcrest Park, full of family-friendly and wheelchair-accessible activities. The zoo provided exhibits of exotic animals with occasional educational shows. Right after Valentine's Day, during such an event, their three resident zebra mares—Sue, Dark, and Crook—attacked their handler, Cecila Marshall.

Martinez read articles that essentially transcribed the events, wherein the zebras started vocalizing before surrounding their experienced zookeeper, who had been with the city-owned zoo for over a decade. While circling, Sue landed a swift kick to the back of the zookeeper's head, killing her instantly, but that was not the most disturbing part of the attack. The three zebras then started biting her, tearing off chunks of flesh. *Whoa! Aren't zebras herbivores?* A shiver ran down Martinez's back; she made a mental note to look up the video of the attack online after she landed.

The animals, still contained within their caged enclosure, were tranquilized by another zookeeper and later put down by animal control. There were op-ed pieces about the safety of small zoos, questions about animal rights, and morbid fascination with the particulars of the attack. That was the reality of media these days—a small spark in one city could circle the globe and ignite all manner of heated issues, regardless how germane they may or may not be to the actual precipitating event.

As for the actual residents of Clovis, the community grieved the passing of their beloved zookeeper, who had made it her home for over fifteen years. The local paper dedicated an entire page to Cecila Ellen Marshall's obituary. Martinez scanned the images, many with animals or loved ones in various locales, but there was one just of Cecila's face. Her brown eyes sparkled with mirth and the delicate lines around her mouth and eyes testified to a life full of laughs. She skimmed the text: age forty-eight; survived by her wife, parents, sister, brother, and a slew of cousins, nephews, and nieces; graduated with her Bachelors and Masters of Animal Sciences from Ohio State University. Her family asked that she be remembered by her love of animals and their conservation, not the circumstances of her death. Martinez held back fat tears welling in her eyes, and the woman next to her silently offered her a tissue. She graciously accepted and composed herself, thankful that Wilson wasn't present to witness such a display.

Martinez shut her phone off and took a breather to walk the aisle with the excuse of using the facilities. She eased herself into the cramped space, used the restroom, and managed to wash her hands without splashing water all over her blouse or jacket. She did a quick check of her makeup and caught her own eye in the reflection. She pressed the amber pendent under her shirt against her skin before returning to her seat. Martinez broke out her packed lunch and watched a brainless episode of some network sitcom that passed as entertainment in the cheap seats. The complimentary drink cart passed just in time for her to get a little caffeine and water.

The woman next to her introduced herself as Nancy, and she was returning home after visiting her first grandbaby. There was no shortage of baby pictures—as was so often the case with grandbabies—and soon Martinez knew more than she ever needed to know about Nancy's daughter and son-in-law. They shared a companionable ten minutes chatting before Martinez returned to her phone, explaining that she was traveling for work and had meetings shortly after landing. Nancy excused her from the conversation and continued with her amusements.

Martinez pulled up the files for the third attack that had occurred just two days ago. Leader had covered the basics in the briefing: five male pronghorns attacked a zookeeper bringing feed into the enclosure during a zoo education session. The animals were tranquilized and quarantined, and the entire Elephant Odyssey section had been closed to visitors for the remainder of the weekend. The injured zookeeper, Marco Estevez, was taken to Scripps Mercy Hospital for emergency surgery and was listed in critical condition.

The San Diego Zoo was one of the most prestigious and popular zoos in the US, home to over 3,500 animals from Asia, Africa, Australia, and the Americas. Privately owned by the nonprofit organization San Diego Zoo Global, the zoo had been in operation for over a hundred years and was considered a leader in its commitment to animal conservation—they were one of the few zoos that had successfully bred a giant panda. Their cageless exhibits sought to recreate natural habitats, allowing animals and visitors a more pleasant zoo experience. Their credentials were impeccable; they belonged to the entire zoological alphabet soup: the Association of Zoos and Aquariums (AZA), the American Alliance of Museums (AAM), the Zoological Association of America (ZAA), and the World Association of Zoos and Aquariums (WAZA). Apart from a few episodes of escaped animals, their pedigree was above reproach until the attack.

Martinez made a few notes in preparation for her appointment with the San Diego zoo director later that afternoon, hopefully followed by access to the animals and their pen. She mulled over the three attacks; the only similarities across the board—besides the appearance of a known Ivory Tower agent—was that all the affected animals were herbivorous ungulates exhibiting aggression in an unconventional mode of attack, with the absence of known triggers for their species. Some, but not all, of the animals were tested for rabies, and she wondered if this was some sort of new disease. If so, was it manufactured or naturally occurring? Was transmission to humans possible?

One thing that niggled at her gut was the escalation in venue. Assuming the events were related, it started at a dinky local petting zoo, stepped up to a small city zoo, and finally to one of the most popular zoos in America—that was like turning the knob from zero to one to eleven. She didn't know if the escalation was deliberate—were the first two attacks practice or testing proof of concept for the more public third attack?—or if it was just coincidence. Martinez ran down the potential methods of external exposure: common suppliers of food, medication, or other animal supplies topped the list. If something was directly introduced into the animals or environment, that could require being on-site before the attack. There could be multiple actors in coordination or a single person that traveled to each site.

The spacing of the attacks suggested a lone perpetrator. Multiple conspirators could coordinate attacks, allowing them to occur at the same time for the greatest impact. Yet the frequency also bothered Martinez. It seemed rushed, compressed—why three attacks in three months? Were there more in the works? She hardly needed to list "magic" in her notes—it was the wild card that could explain the unfathomable. Martinez shut her eyes and let everything percolate in her brain while the Budos Band streamed in through her earbuds. She sighed, hoping Wilson was having better luck with the files, before moving onto the Ivory Tower primer Chloe and Dot put on her phone.

*****

Wilson sipped his tomato juice and stretched out in his spacious seat, enjoying the extra legroom that his five and a half feet didn't really warrant—it made it all the more decadent. His cover was Davis Watson, your average white-collar man in chinos and a polo, escaping the shitty Michigan weather to spend some time in sunny SoCal eating tacos and churros. The fact that he was buried intently in the phone for hours at a time was no different than everyone else on the plane. Optics were everything.

He reviewed the files Leader provided on the three attacks and found himself taking another look at the photos of Lukin. Now somewhere in his late fifties, he'd aged since they'd last crossed paths five years ago. Wilson loathed to admit that his roguish good looks had matured into a worldly charm—no doubt if Ivory Tower was handing out codenames now, he would be Silver Fox.

Despite his name and nationality, Sasha was ethnically German; his parents fled Berlin at the end of WWII and used their knowledge as a bargaining chip in the new world order. The Soviet Union welcomed them and whitewashed their past, giving them Russian papers and names—not unlike Operation Paperclip, the US military initiative that brought Nazi scientists into America and sheltered them from justice for their war crimes, in exchange for their knowledge of the German warfare innovations and future contributions to US military tech. Only the Lukins didn't know anything about technology; they were practitioners of the magical arts.

The Russians have always had a love affair with magic—it's seeped into their bones, deeper than any expressed conscious ideology. But despite this predilection, much of what they considered "magic" was hokum, the original opium of their masses. Under the Lukins' hands, the Ivory Tower was born—as was Sasha, an unexpected late-in-life arrival. Born and raised under the hammer and sickle, he was Russian through and through, despite his blue eyes and blond hair.

If there was one thing the Soviets had in spades, it was people, and Ivory Tower agents were plentiful and disposable. The Tower didn't care about karmic cost or careful management of resources; they would simply recruit a new batch of good-enoughs and send them out to do the bidding of the Interior Council—the committee that governed their magical assets. But Sasha was different; he was their son, and they were not Soviet in their hearts of hearts—there was still room for sentimentality. They trained Sasha as a true magician, granting him the skills, knowledge, and competency to survive the fall of the USSR, mission after mission, and the death of his parents. Whatever was going on, it had to be of some importance to send one of their most experienced agents.

Wilson enlarged the picture on his screen with an outward burst of his thumb and forefinger, zooming in on his quarry. He stared at the picture for a long time, burning his enemy's aged face into memory.

Chapter Five

San Diego, California, USA
1st of April, 4:10 p.m. (GMT-7)

Charlotte Dumont retreated to her office on the top floor of the administrative heart of the San Diego Zoo after the latest spate of meetings and interviews, and collapsed into her chair. The past forty-eight hours had been a nonstop whirlwind of activity: statements to the press, interviews that aired on local and national news, and carefully worded tweets—vigorously vetted by their public relations department to remind everyone of the zoo's commitment to the safety and wellbeing of the animals, staff, and patrons without sounding tone-deaf. An animal attack was every zoo director's nightmare—the only way it could have been worse was if a zoo guest or volunteer had been attacked.

This morning, she reassured the panicked board of directors that safety protocols had been followed and department heads were already starting the necessary audits—both for the zoo's benefit as well as to appease the larger community of responsible zoos and aquariums. The zoo expressed heartfelt well wishes for Zookeeper Estevez's speedy recovery, but that didn't stop California's Division of Occupational Safety and Health from opening a formal investigation "to determine whether or not any occupational safety and health standards were violated and/or contributed to the incident." They inspected the work area and requested a mountain of paperwork as proof of employer due-diligence—work schedules, vaccinations, TB checks, safety protocols, and staff training of said protocols, to start.

And then there was the matter of what to do with the animals—some were requesting they be put down, others used this tragedy to call for animal freedom and rally against the "zoo establishment." The zoo was not required to immunize the pronghorns against rabies since they were permanent residents and not exposed to wild animals, but thankfully Mr. Estevez was vaccinated. According to guidelines, a ten-day observation period could be used to rule out the risk of potential rabies exposure to humans as long as the animal had a low probability of rabies. Within hours after the attack, she had set up a quarantine for observation and had the exhibit and pens scrubbed per protocol.

Unfortunately, the pronghorns became aggressive as soon as the sedatives wore off and refused their normal food. This deviant behavior could not go uninvestigated, and with a heavy heart, Dumont agreed to surrender the animals for euthanasia and testing for rabies. While the test only took twenty-four to seventy-two hours, it required killing the animal to obtain at least two samples of brain tissue—one from the brain stem and another from the cerebellum—and not all facilities had the setup for that kind of precise extraction and tissue preparation. The closest processor was in Los Angeles. The lab at UCLA had agreed to perform the tests, but the technicians didn't work on weekends. Dumont accordingly arranged for transport today after the zoo closed.

And now, as if she didn't have enough on her plate, the FBI wanted to see her. She had just enough time to use the restroom and take something for the headache that had been looming over her all day. A crisp knock fell on her door at precisely 4:15 p.m., and her assistant brought in the visitor. A solid woman in a dark gray suit emerged through the doorway. Wide in the shoulders and hips, the slightly crumpled suit framed the tall agent while she provided her identification for Dumont. "Hello, I am Special Agent Martinez from the Federal Bureau of Investigations. Dr. Dumont?" Dumont scanned the badge and photo ID; the picture matched the brunette in front of her.

A bob of the director's head indicated she was satisfied with Martinez's credentials, and Martinez tucked away her ID in the inner pocket of her suit. "That's me," Dumont answered, and extended her right hand. "I am Charlotte Dumont, director of the San Diego Zoo."

Martinez shook her hand and did a quick assessment of the woman in front of her. Somewhere in her late forties, Charlotte Dumont was impeccably dressed in a sleek Armani suit and Prada pin-heeled Mary Janes. She carried herself with poise, and her posture and demeanor projected power. She armed herself with her polished appearance: her manicured hands, flawless makeup, and styled hair all declared this was not a person to be trifled with.

Dr. Dumont's assessment of Martinez was less thorough—a firm handshake and steely brown eyes indicated she was a serious person who wasn't going to waste her time. Dr. Dumont smiled and motioned to a leather couch to one side of the room. "Please, take a seat. Can I offer you anything to drink? Coffee, tea, water?"

Martinez politely declined and did a quick visual sweep before sitting. Dr. Dumont's corner office was spacious with a wraparound desk tucked to one side, granting the director unfettered views of the zoo below from the bank of windows. In addition to a computer and organizational materials, there were obligatory family photos on the desktop. Three framed diplomas hung on the wall behind it, calligraphic evidence of Dr. Dumont's academic achievements strategically placed where one could not help but see them if they were addressing her at her desk. A full-sized bookshelf stood against the nearby wall bearing folders, tomes, and tasteful animal-themed arts and crafts.

"That will be all, Melissa." Dumont nodded her curious secretary out of the office. "Please, close the door behind you and hold all calls." Dr. Dumont heavily sat down in her chair. "How can I be of assistance to the FBI?"

"We are interested in the attack that occurred two days ago

and would appreciate San Diego Zoo's full cooperation in our investigation," Martinez stated plainly. "We'd like to start by asking you and your staff some questions, take a look at the site of the attack and the security video, and obtain a list of suppliers and recent changes in personnel."

Dr. Dumont was taken aback by the request. "This sounds rather serious for what was an unfortunate accident, albeit a tragic one. However, I'm more than happy to answer any questions you have and give you access to the zoo's property. Naturally, I'll have to check with our legal department before surrendering any information on our employees. May I ask what piqued the FBI's interest in this matter?"

Martinez met her curious gaze. "Animal attacks with a similar profile have recently occurred at other zoos in the US. We need to determine if they are independent events or somehow related."

"Other zoos?" Dumont inquired with genuine surprise. She was unaware of any similar attacks.

"Happy Farm Petting Zoo in Tempe, Arizona, and Hillcrest Park Zoo in Clovis, New Mexico," Martinez rattled off without having to consult her phone—a fact that did not go unnoticed by Dr. Dumont—and she paused to see if the names meant anything to the director, to no avail. "Much smaller operations, compared to the San Diego Zoo," she continued, "but all involved herbivorous ungulates attacking people. That is why we are requesting suppliers and staff related to the pronghorns—to cross-reference with the other institutions to rule out any type of accidental exposure."

"Accidental…" Dumont grasped the implication of what Martinez had elided. "Does that mean the FBI thinks it is possible this attack was orchestrated?"

Martinez kept her face neutral, but appreciated the director's facile mind. "It's early days, and we are investigating all possibilities." She leaned in. "Did you or the zoo receive any threatening communications preceding the attack?"

Dumont's brow furrowed and she looked side to side, the first hint of a crack in her professional demeanor since Martinez had entered her office. "There is always a fringe element that objects to zoos on philosophical or ethical grounds, but I'm not aware of a recent uptick from the anti-zoo fundamentalists. Quite frankly, the zoo has a great reputation in animal care and conservation efforts, and we have a lot of community support—over half a million members."

"Any disgruntled employees that were let go in the past six months, or recent hires in the past six weeks that have failed to come into work since the incident?"

Dumont glanced at her wristwatch. "Our HR director is gone for the day, but I could certainly ask her to speak to you tomorrow." Martinez pulled out her phone to make notes. "Ms. Diana Hartfield," the director added.

Martinez's fingers swiftly tapped over her screen without looking down. "Would it be possible to take a look at the enclosure and pens this afternoon? Perhaps meet with security?"

Dumont picked up her phone and pressed two buttons. "Melissa—please call Brandon to escort Agent Martinez to Elephant Odyssey, and see who is working security today. Also, make an appointment for Agent Martinez with Ms. Hartfield for tomorrow morning." Martinez heard the indistinct garble of a reply through the phone. Dumont set down the receiver and paused before speaking. "It doesn't make any sense; I could understand if it was a bomb threat, a shooting, a protest, or even an attack on our website—we have a lot of online traffic on our zoo cams, and a sizable amount of our ticket sales are made online as well. But if this was deliberate, that would mean biological sabotage—something that would affect the animals."

"As I said before, we are considering all angles," Martinez spoke matter-of-factly before lightening her mood and nodding to the diplomas behind the director. "I see you're a Buckeye?"

The distracted director blinked back into the conversation and half-turned her head until she realized what Agent Martinez was referring to. "OH-IO," she chanted the call-and-response with a smile. "A long time ago. I miss it sometimes," she said with a nostalgic smile, "but I don't miss Ohio winters."

*****

Wilson slowly walked the path through Elephant Odyssey,

getting a lay of the terrain, noting the security cameras and the entrances into the restricted areas. Today was the first day this section was open to the public since the attack, and traffic was busy. The pronghorn exhibit was obscured with scrims but that didn't stop people from approaching and whispering, drawn to tragedy like flies to dung. He bought a bag of overpriced roasted nuts and took a seat watching the elephants with the closed exhibit in his periphery. He wore a hat, wig, and sunglasses, and kept watch for Lukin. His disguise was complete with some cheap zoo-branded clothing for which he'd paid not-so-cheap prices. Anyone who might recognize him would never believe he'd dress so tackily.

His phone vibrated in his pocket—a text from Martinez. *Poss cnx. Cecila Marshall and Charlotte Dumont nee Kendall. Both did graduate work at Ohio State during mid-90s. SM dig?*

Wilson tapped out a terse reply. *K. Access?*

Martinez: *To pen - will salt. L8r security for video. Appt w/ HR tmrw am. L?*

No sign. Wilson tapped out. He stood and made another circuit while his phone dialed the Salt Mine's outside line.

"Discretion Minerals, how may I direct your call?" a friendly female voice chimed from the other end of the line.

"This is Davis Watson, calling for my messages." He skirted the edge of gawkers.

"Good evening, Mr. Watson. How is the weather?"

"Fine, but it could turn at any moment."

The operator moved to the next set of questions. "And the food?"

"A little too spicy for my taste but palatable." Wilson spied a quiet nook away from the crowd.

"Any souvenirs?"

"Just a shirt that says 'I'm with stupid.'"

"One moment." The line went silent as Wilson found a spot in a quiet nook behind some overgrown foliage in the relatively secluded spot at the far end of the elephant care center.

A clipped male voice picked up the line, "Good evening, Fulcrum. Search parameters?"

"Cecila Marshall and Charlotte Dumont, maiden name Kendall, Ohio State University in the mid-90s." The voice repeated back the information, and the line went dead once he obtained Wilson's confirmation.

Wilson emerged from his hidey-hole and blended into a group of people exiting the elephant care center. He returned to his previous lookout, but had to pass the bench entirely as it was currently occupied by none other than one Alexander Petrovich Lukin.

*****

"Well, that's it—you've seen everything behind the scenes," the strapping head zookeeper declared with a heavy Australian accent. It made Martinez's insides flutter in a way that was unhelpful in the middle of an investigation.

"Thank you for the tour, Mr. Evans," Martinez replied.

"Please, call me Brandon." He gave her a broad smile that went all the way to his baby blues. "Is there anything else you would like to see? Dr. Dumont instructed me to show you whatever you wanted." The double entendre was killing her.

"I would like a peek at the actual enclosure, even though it's been cleaned. It was covered on my way in."

"Sure, right this way." He motioned with an outstretched arm as a disembodied voice shouted from behind them.

"Brandon, where is the paperwork for the transport team?"

"It's in the blue folder, in the outgoing box," he answered back.

"No, it's not," the faceless speaker countered.

Brandon sighed. "Did you even look?"

"Of course. That's how I know it's not there."

Brandon placed a hand on Martinez's back, guiding her in the general direction. "It's right through that door. It has a two-latch system that opens on the inside—simple for humans to operate, but not so much hoofed animals." He winked at her before going deeper into the building.

Martinez slipped into the enclosure and oriented herself, matching the physical space with the video of the attack posted online. She pulled out her vape pen-cum-saltcaster, lined up the notches, pressed the button, and started with the path of attack. A short blow dispersed a thin mist of salt; Martinez held her breath. She waited for the salt to settle, but no design emerged. She tried again at the privacy lean-to where the animals could retreat when the ogling masses got to them, but there was no sign of magical activity. She moved to the watering hole where food was placed—if something supernatural was added to their intake, there could be traces of it still. Martinez loosed another wave of salt and watched intently, but again nothing shifted.

She clicked her e-cigarette back to normal when she heard the latch engage behind her. "Sorry to leave you on your own," Brandon apologized. He flipped his eyes to her vape pen. "You smoke?"

"Trying to quit," she sheepishly replied as she tucked the device away. "It's harder than it looks."

"Well, good for you," he spoke with enthusiastic encouragement. "Can't quit if you don't try. If you're done here, I can walk you over to security."

Martinez gave a final panoramic look. "I think I've got everything I need here."

Chapter Six

San Diego, California, USA
1ˢᵗ of April, 5:00 p.m. (GMT-7)

Alexander Petrovich Lukin was so tired of America; more specifically, Americans. They talked too much and too loudly. They were boorish and utterly exhausting. When he was first assigned the mission, he was pleased at the prospect of spending winter in warmer climes, but the novelty of the American southwest was wearing thin. It did not help that he had spent the past three months in numerous zoos; he was certain it brought out the worst in families. And then there was the relentless sunshine and warmth; he dreamt of snowy days spent curled up with a warm bowl of Solyanka, a decent loaf of bread, and a good bottle of vodka. It was unnatural to wear shorts in March.

He took a seat in the newly reopened Elephant Odyssey and waited for his moment—today was his last chance of obtaining a blood sample with minimal difficulty. Normally, Lukin preferred to maneuver in the cover of night when security would be at its most lax, but that was not possible, if his intel was correct. The pronghorns would be moved shortly after zoo closing for extermination and testing.

According to his surveillance, the final hour before closing was his best bet, when the zookeepers would be preoccupied caring for the other animals, leaving the recently sedated pronghorns alone. It was a simple plan: he would jam the cameras, slip into the bay where the pronghorns were quarantined, perform a little venipuncture, and be out before the zoo closed its gates. He just had to be patient.

Nearby, a petulant child was screaming, insisting that his sister had a bigger ice cream than him. In a fit of rage, the boy swatted his sister's hand, knocking the treat to the ground. His crocodile tears ceased and a self-satisfied grin spread on his face as she registered her loss and wailed. Lukin sardonically laughed—that was the nature of things, programmed so deeply that even children knew the honest state of affairs.

It was nearing time, and Lukin rose from the bench. He meandered out of Elephant Odyssey and onto the main road, creatively called "Bus Road." He walked the gently curving slope and waited for a trolley full of people to pass before cutting into the backside of the enclosure past the sign painted "restricted access—zoo vehicles only."

Lukin swiped the keycard he had pocketed off a janitor earlier that afternoon and slid through the back door. He heard voices within and took cover behind a low wall. "After you, Agent Martinez," a thick Australian accent came from the other side of the partition. He stayed perfectly still until he heard the door he had just entered open and shut. Yet another reason Lukin had hoped to wait—the place had been crawling with press, zoo personnel, and inspectors.

He slipped on a pair of gray coveralls hanging on the wall, seeped with the musty smell of animals, hay, and sweat. He had no qualms using magic, but there hardly seemed the need—the correct uniform was excellent camouflage. He maneuvered through the concrete building with ease and readied a spell as he neared the office. Lukin glided across the doorway where an overworked and underpaid peon typed on an ancient computer and shuffled paperwork while listening to death metal through his earbuds. He could hear the thrashing from the hallway and let his incipient spell drop.

Lukin waited until he was almost at the pen before he scrambled the camera—he didn't want to attract attention from the metalhead but he also didn't want his face captured on the quarantine cam. The pronghorns were on the ground, their legs collapsed under their bodies. They didn't rouse at his approach and their glazed look was consistent with sedation, but he didn't like the way their dark bulbous eyes tracked him.

He murmured in Russian, weaving his words into a gentle cadence, lulling the animals into a trance-like state. The nearest pronghorn lowered its head, presenting its neck. Its jugular vein pulsed against the taut flesh. He donned gloves, pulled out an eighteen-gauge needle, and readied the first of four tubes. He continued the incantation as he pierced the animal's neck, guiding it into the vein. Once he saw the flashback, he popped the first tube and it filled with crimson. There was a flicker of resistance in the pronghorn's eyes, but Lukin's song soothed it back into peaceful oblivion. He filled the remaining three tubes in series before withdrawing the needle and dropping it into a nearby sharps container filled with the needles used to sedate the animals.

Lukin retraced his steps, turning off his scrambling device once he was clear of the cameras. He shed the coveralls where he found them, hoping the zoo funk hadn't bled into his own clothes. He wiped his prints off the access card and dropped it on the ground—no more visits to San Diego Zoo for him. He carefully removed his gloves and used them to cushion the glass vials of blood, which he carefully placed in the pockets of his American cargo shorts. Lukin pushed the door open with his back, pulled out his sunglasses, and deftly merged into visitor traffic. The lowering light of early evening colored the blue sky in streaks of pinkish orange, and a cool breeze stirred the warm air. He was so pleased with the operation, he was none the wiser that he had picked up a shadow.

*****

Wilson hated traffic, but he found solace knowing that Lukin was stuck in it three cars ahead of him and in a shittier rental car. Wilson flipped his phone off silent mode now that he was no longer following him on foot and found a new text from Martinez. *Salt neg. @ htl rm w/ videos.*

He sent off a quick reply. *Dig started, on L, SYL.*

Martinez replied almost immediately. *Be careful.* Wilson found himself smiling in the rear view mirror; she didn't even abbreviate—she must have finished reading Lukin's file.

Wilson joined the caravan of cars abandoning the highway for city streets, keeping a respectful distance from Lukin's lightning-blue Ford Fiesta as it headed north across the river. The Russian pulled into a shopping center that was home to a handful of restaurants, clothing stores, and a twenty-four-hour retail shipping company. Wilson glided out from behind him and veered left, pulling into a spot in the adjacent block but within eyesight of Lukin's car, now parked in front of the shipping store.

Wilson watched him hustle indoors with a small box. The wide exterior windows allowed Wilson a full view of what appeared to be a minor exchange of words, as Lukin started using his hands while he spoke and the clerk took a step back from the angry Russian. Wilson noted the time: 7:30 p.m. Lukin left the store without the package and drove to a respectable mid-price hotel—the kind of place that doesn't have room service, but does offer a warm complimentary breakfast.

Wilson watched the windows in the front and started counting from the moment Lukin entered the front door, waiting for one of the dark rectangles to light up. It was a fifty-

fifty shot—Lukin's room could have been facing the back—but it was better than nothing. It took two minutes for the edges of the third window from the north end on the third floor to flicker to life behind its closed curtain. Satisfied for now with his reasonable guess regarding Lukin's sleeping arraignments, Wilson fired up his BMW and pulled away. He had work to do.

The parking lot in front of the twenty-four-hour shipping center was empty, as most of the vehicles huddled around the eateries at this time of night. The neon lights glowed in the window of the otherwise empty showroom. Wilson ditched the zoo paraphernalia but left the rest of his disguise on—he could charm the clerk but not the cameras. Before he left his car, he started his spell, repeating a mantra from a book his mother use to read to him as a child: *think, think, think.*

The electronic chime sounded as he entered the store, and the clerk was typing away on his keyboard, giving Wilson a little more time to power his magic. "Excuse me, I was in here just a little while ago," Wilson spoke in his voice, but the clerk heard a familiar Russian accent instead.

The lone employee apologized without looking up, "I'm sorry you missed the last pickup for the night, but I'm sending it out first thing tomorrow. That's the best I can do."

"I think I've found a place that can ship it out tonight," Wilson infused more enchantment in his words. "If you could give me back my package, I'll be on my way."

The clerk looked up from his screen, his mind adding five inches in height and forty pounds of bulk—whatever it took for him to be convinced that it was Lukin standing in front of him once again. "I doubt there is a place nearby, but you're more than welcome to try."

Wilson shrugged. "I can always return if I'm wrong—you're open all night."

The clerk matched his gesture. "Sure. Where's your receipt?"

Wilson patted down his pockets, feigning a search. "I seem to have misplaced it, but you checked me out less than an hour ago. Help a guy out?" Wilson interlaced more suggestion in his tone.

The clerk sighed and turned around. He fished out a square box from the top of the stack and brought it to the counter. "I didn't do this."

Wilson smiled. "Understood. I really appreciate it."

It was almost 9:00 p.m. by the time he returned to his hotel after a short stop for takeout. It was going to be a long night, and he hadn't eaten in hours. The do-not-disturb sign was still in place as he let himself into his room. He turned on the light and checked for evidence of tampering. Satisfied everything was as he left it, he settled into a chair and texted Martinez: *@ hotel.* He was unaccustomed to checking in with anyone, but felt it was the right thing to do under the circumstances. Martinez reply was simply *K.*

Wilson devoured a container of beef flat noodles before

turning his attention to Lukin's package. He donned gloves before examining the label, noting its final destination. He carefully sliced the packing tape on the bottom of the box, leaving the original shipping label intact, and he preserved as much of the packing material as possible before unearthing the four vials of blood. He inverted the vials and found them still fluid, despite the hours passed. *That's odd—the blood should have congealed by now.*

Wilson retrieved a ruler, string, and blue chalk from his suitcase and cleared the floor of his bathroom of towels and mats. He methodically marked two interlocking triangles forming the body of a six-pointed star. Pinning one end of the string in its center, he drew a circle around the star, making sure each point touched the arc. He fastidiously wrote symbols in the space captured at the star's points, making sure they connected all three sides of the smaller triangle within, before popping the top of one of the vials and pouring a dollop of blood in the center of the star.

Wilson chanted, calling a minor entity to aid him—one of the first Chloe and Dot had taught him to summon. It didn't take long for a blothis to appear, hovering above the space bound by the circle on the floor. It may have been a small, winged ethereal creature, but there wasn't anything Tinkerbell about it. It was a foul-mouthed imp with grotesque facial features and a vicious toothy maw that wanted to know why it was being summoned.

"Oh great blothis, I ask a small thing and make offering for your vast knowledge," Wilson loftily hailed his guest. It may be small in stature, but it was mighty in ego.

Sufficiently supplicated, the blothis entertained Wilson's presence. "What is it you seek?"

Wilson bowed slightly. "To know the nature of magic upon the blood before you."

"And the offering?" it petulantly inquired, seeing nothing else within the circle.

"I am but a humble seeker of truth. All I have to offer is the blood itself," Wilson played up his wretchedness.

It sniffed the glob of blood and smacked its lips. "It is an unworthy offering, but I will take pity on your lowly self." Agreement reached, the blothis dove down and slurped the viscous goo. Its belly swelled and it let out a laugh. "You truly are slow. There is no magic in this except of preservation. It's like drinking it straight from the vein."

Wilson thanked the creature for its wisdom, and dismissed it back to its realm. Wilson's brow furrowed as he wiped away the summoning circle—he thought for certain there was something supernatural about the blood. Why else would Lukin cross the Atlantic to obtain it? Leader's directive was clear—if Lukin wanted something, Wilson was to get it first, but without detection.

Wilson assembled a new box and packed the unopened three vials—with judicious padding—labeling the package for the Salt Mine lab; it might not be magic—at least, by the blood imp's reckoning—but it was still worth investigating if the Ivory Tower wanted it so badly. Wilson unscrewed the back of his compass and placed one drop of the blood in the chamber. There was little doubt in Wilson's mind that Lukin cast the spell to preserve the blood, and this should give him some way of keeping track of his movements when nearby but out-of-sight. Carefully putting the top back on the half-empty tube, he initiated part two of his scheme.

Using his phone, he searched for the nearest veterinarian that was outside the city and far from a local sheriff's office. There were numerous pet and animal hospitals littering the area, but the agent opted for a rural private practice that didn't look like it doubled as a residence on street view. It meant a longer drive, but he felt it was worth the effort to avoid security, witnesses, and inevitable questions—who shows up at a pet hospital without an animal?

With the sun finally set, the moist sea air cooled the night, and the road congestion had dissipated. Wilson mapped his route mentally, stopping by another twenty-four-hour shipping company to mail his package to the Salt Mine. Davis Watson made another call to Discretion Minerals, this time to leave a message for his secretary; once he cleared his security questions, he recited the tracking number.

Using his phone's GPS instead of the rental car's, Wilson ventured out of town until the street turned into a two-lane country road. There was a turn off onto a long gravel driveway that led to a single-story building with a barn behind it. The sign in front confirmed it was *Chet the Country Vet's* office. He did a circle in the parking lot, scouting out the terrain, nearby structures, external security cameras, or motion-sensor lights. Once Wilson felt confident in his risk assessment, he killed the engine and turned on his electronic jammer for whatever might be inside the building.

Donning a pair of gloves before softly testing the door, he pulled out a lock pick card from his wallet, freed two ends, and deftly unlocked it. Along the wall near the door, he spotted a newer smart alarm system—the kind that contacts the owner's phone when triggered…were it not currently being jammed, that is. Wilson activated his phone and placed it on top of the unit, buying him more mobility beyond the scrambler's ten meters.

A quick search of the cabinets revealed all the supplies he required: syringes, needles, test tubes, and treats. Threatening barks and rattling collars and cages sounded as Wilson edged down the dark hallway with just the dim beam of his small flashlight lighting the way. He smiled as his good fortune— Chet's overnight guests would save him time and effort.

Wilson started reciting an old nursery rhyme, spinning magic in its lilting pitch, before opening the door to the holding pens. A quick sweep revealed no outside windows to give away his presence, and the animals' fear quelled and their yips quieted under his song. He closed the door behind him and swapped his flashlight for the overhead fluorescents.

Moving slowly as to not to rile the animals, he considered his options. Wilson began singing "This Old Man" as he focused on a beagle. The dog's soulful brown eyes were fully entranced by the time the old man gave the dog his first bone. When he opened the cage, the dog greeted him like an old friend, accepting pets and scratches around his floppy ears like they'd known each other for years.

Wilson started on the second verse while he positioned the dog on the table, holding his front leg in one hand with slight pressure and rotation. He wiped down the area with alcohol—no need to risk an infection that could draw attention to the animal—and waited for the cephalic vein to fill. Once it became plump and easily palpable, Wilson put a little more charm into the next verse before sticking the dog with the needle. He drew back, filling the syringe before grabbing another, keenly aware that he had to have enough to fill four tubes. The beagle whimpered on the second stick but didn't pull away or bite.

Wilson withdrew the second needle and continued his song, gently petting the beagle and scratching behind its ears again. Safely returned to his cage, Wilson slipped in a few dog treats he had found stashed behind the reception desk. The beagle perked up.

Wilson injected the dog's blood into the four tubes. Then he took a clean needle and drew up the remaining pronghorn's blood, placing a few drops in each tube—enough to preserve the sample while still bearing Lukin's magical signature should anyone check. He deposited the needles in the sharps bins and the syringes and unused blood into the biohazard bin. This old man had played ten by the time Wilson turned off the lights, picked up his phone, relocked the front door, and got back into his car.

It was close to one in the morning by the time he got back into town. He deposited Lukin's repacked and resealed package at the drop box rather than return to the storefront, and he stopped by Lukin's hotel and circled the parking lot. The crappy Ford Fiesta was in the same place, and Wilson's compass needle was pointing true. He quickly parked and slid a tracer under the rear bumper.

By the time Wilson dragged himself back to his hotel room, the rush had passed and he was dead tired. He picked up his fortune cookie from dinner and cracked it open—cookies are for closers, and he deemed today a success. He bit into the crunchy sweet shell as he read the slip of paper: *Appearances can be deceiving.* Wilson let out a snort.

Chapter Seven

San Diego, California, USA
2nd of April, 5:00 a.m. (GMT-7)

Martinez had set the alarm on her phone before bed, but figured she wouldn't need it with the time difference—after all, her meeting with Diana Hartfield wasn't until 9:30 a.m. She'd spent the bulk of the evening watching the footage zoo security had copied for her, but there was only so long she could concentrate on the screen. She'd managed to eek out two extra hours of sleep before her internal clock kicked in, triggering an instant panic that she had overslept the alarm. Of course, it was only 5:00 a.m. Pacific Time, which would have been an ungodly hour five months ago when she was still stationed at the FBI's Portland Field Office. There was only a three hour difference between Detroit and San Diego—not enough to cause jet lag, but enough to seriously mess with one's day.

She might have gone back to sleep, but she made the mistake of checking her phone and discovered an email from the Salt Mine: Connection confirmed—Charlotte Kendall, Cecila Marshall, and Milo Perkins did graduate work in the same department at OSU '93-'95. Martinez's mind started spinning—there was no chance she was going back to sleep now.

She immediately opened the first attachment, a screenshot from the OSU yearbook, the Makio. It was a club listing for the American Association of Zoo Veterinarians: Cecila Marshall was the vice president and Charlotte Kendall was the treasurer. "They definitely knew each other," Martinez muttered to herself as she rose and started a cup of hotel room coffee on her way to the bathroom.

She scanned the second attachment with one hand while nursing her hot beverage with the other. It was an academic paper titled "Building a Better Zoo: A Multifactorial Approach to Reduce Animal Distress in Captivity." The list of authors was long enough to warrant an "et al." if cited, but Martinez stopped once she saw C. Marshall and M. Perkins credited. The gears in her brain started turning once the caffeine percolated into her system. *Interesting…Milo and Cecila worked together academically.*

The final attachment was two pages from *The Lantern*, OSU's student newspaper, announcing that renovations in the Animal Sciences building were complete. The article quoted Charlotte Kendall, graduate researcher in animal sciences, on how vital the new lab and equipment were to "maintaining OSU's position as a research institution in the field." Martinez smiled—even in her twenties, Dr. Dumont knew how to put her best foot forward. The splash page featured a picture of four people in white lab coats spelling out the hallmark "O-H-I-O" with their arms.

Martinez sat up. *I've seen that picture before. Where have I seen that picture?* She shuffled icons on her screen and opened the case files she'd read on the plane, until she came to Cecila Marshall's obituary. There it was, sandwiched between a picture of Cecila with a giraffe and a photo of her at her commencement. Martinez zoomed in and examined the faces. She was pretty sure the first "O" was Cecila, and the "I" could be a younger Dr. Dumont, but who were the two men on either side of them?

Martinez returned to *The Lantern*, hoping they cited the people in the photo, but the caption was less than enlightening: "Graduate students christen new lab, Buckeye style." Martinez fired up her laptop and started the hunt for pictures of Milo Perkins. The internet and social media made this kind of work much easier, and the problem was typically one of too much data. Without more information, it was hard to figure out which Milo Perkins was the one she was looking for, which was why Salt Mine agents generally left the sifting to the analysts— separating the wheat from the chaff was their forte. Luckily, this Milo Perkins had recently been in the news.

Once Martinez found a recent picture of him, it was easy to pick him out of the many Milo Perkinses on social media. The next hurdle was his age; he was of a generation that grew up before e-mail, the internet, or smart phones. Any photos from that time would have been uploaded from physical pictures. Martinez went down the rabbit hole, going through all his friends and groups until she found some OSU alumni. Martinez silently thanked throwback Thursday—#tbt—as it eventually found a contemporary picture of him with more hair and less love handles for comparison. There was little doubt in Martinez's mind that Milo Perkins was the "H." Which begged the question, who was the second "O?" Martinez knew just the person to ask, once it was a decent hour.

*****

Wilson grabbed his buzzing phone and cursed under his breath; he vowed that one day soon, he would get a full night's sleep. It took him a second to orient himself in space and time as he rolled under the comforter and glanced at the clock—7:00 a.m. Without getting up, he swiped his phone and found the analysts had been hard at work—there was a communication from the Salt Mine with an attachment, but that wasn't what caused his phone to stir. Martinez had messaged him. *U up?*

He tapped back. *I am now. Problem?*

Martinez: *No, but need to swap info.*

Wilson weighed his options. Salt Mine agents typically worked solo, so there wasn't a mission protocol for this. Technically, Martinez was supposed to be the public face of the investigation, but there was little point in sending two agents if they couldn't share intel. They weren't supposed to be seen together, but Wilson reasoned that it should be okay to meet as long as they stayed out of public purview. *Rm 537. Give me 20 mins to shower.*

Martinez: *K. I'll bring breakfast.*

Wilson locked his phone and threw back the covers—he was officially on the clock now and Martinez hadn't been late yet. He regarded the stubble on his face—Davis Watson was on vacation; he could forgo that S but the other two could not be ignored. After he used the toilet, he cranked on the hot water and gave the hotel toiletries a sniff. Once, he had forgotten to check and spent a regrettable day smelling of cucumber melon. The honey almond was acceptable, and Wilson lathered up, letting the weight of the water pound down on him. The steamy shower cleared the sleepy haze from his mind, and what he'd thought of as an unmitigated success last night seemed less clear-cut in the morning light. He was unable to shake the notion he was missing something; if the blood had been magical in its own right, Wilson would have felt better about the whole thing.

His stomach growled as he turned off the water and toweled himself dry; a cold rush hit him as he opened the door and released the steam from the bathroom. Wilson started coffee on the single cup machine as he hastily dressed.

He had just finished when a crisp knock landed on his door; Wilson stepped up to the peephole and saw Martinez through the fish-eyed lens. "Hope you like breakfast tacos," she greeted him, handing over a warm unmarked brown bag. The smell was heavenly.

"Only monsters don't like breakfast tacos," he replied after shutting the door. He took the bag to the table where his coffee was waiting for him, and unwrapped the first silvery torpedo. "So, what did you find out?"

Martinez took a seat and filled him in while he ate. "The zoo director denies recent threats to the zoo and has her doubts about this being a deliberate attack, but is playing nice. I spoke to the head zookeeper—nothing unusual or out of the ordinary in the weeks preceding the attack, but Mr. Estevez would be a better person to ask if he wakes up. Apparently, he was the one mainly in charge of the day-to-day care in the camel and pronghorn enclosures. I called the hospital this morning; he's no longer listed as critical, but still hasn't regained consciousness. Nothing magical came up in the enclosure, but I wasn't able to get a moment alone to salt the pronghorns." She sipped her Americano before continuing—head and shoulders above hotel room coffee.

"Security provided me a copy of their surveillance video, with footage up to one week before the attack as well as the days following. I found Lukin on the footage—he was all over the zoo in the days preceding the attack, but once it occurred, he kept hovering near Elephant Odyssey, even when it was closed."

"That's where I picked him up yesterday," Wilson interjected. "He snuck into the building behind the enclosure and obtained blood samples, which ended up only having his magic on it to preserve them—no other magical traces."

"Why would an Ivory Tower agent be after non-magical blood samples?" Martinez wondered.

"Not sure, but they don't have it anymore. I swapped them out, and the original samples are headed to Salt Mine as we speak." Wilson collapsed the aluminum foil into a silver ball and made a free throw into the wastebasket against the opposite wall. "But it does suggest that Lukin isn't working with perfect knowledge. He knew where to be, but didn't know which animals would be affected or when. It was almost six weeks between the second and third attacks—why wait six weeks if you know exactly what you are looking for? For whatever reason, he choose to wait for the third attack to occur," Wilson speculated as he unwrapped his second taco and picked up the salsa verde this time.

"Have you had a chance to look at what the Salt Mine sent?" Martinez asked. Wilson shook his head, too enamored with the chorizo and egg to speak. "They confirmed the OSU connection between all three attacks. I'm going to ask Dr. Dumont some follow-up questions, while I'm there seeing HR to ask about disgruntled fires and new hires. They moved the pronghorns yesterday evening for extermination and rabies testing, so unless the injured zookeeper wakes up, there really isn't much more we need here. I have no problem continuing the investigation, but right now, it doesn't look like there is anything supernatural about it *except* for Lukin. Could this be one of those times an Ivory Tower agent was sent for a mundane mission?"

"Possibly," Wilson stated equivocally and pulled up an address on his phone, "but he did sent it to a lab that the Ivory Tower has been known to use. My ruse bought us some time, but if they have the ability to do DNA testing on the blood, it won't be hard for them to figure out it's dog blood and not pronghorn. We need to figure out whatever Lukin was chasing, and find it first. I'm using Weber's compass to track Lukin's magical signature and also slipped a tracer on his rental car last night. If you can use your badge to get the alias he's traveling under, we can keep closer tabs on him while he's in the US."

"Where do you need me to flash my badge?" she drily queried; she'd known him long enough not to ask where he got dog blood.

"I figured out where he's staying, but I don't want to spook him. I do, however, have the plates of the Ford Fiesta he's renting and it shouldn't be hard to get a name from that on the down low."

Martinez chuckled at Wilson's attempt at slang. "Text it to me, and I'll look into it."

Chapter Eight

San Diego, California, USA
2nd of April, 9:45 a.m. (GMT-7)

The San Diego Zoo employed nearly 3,000 people, but Diana Hartfield couldn't think of anyone with an axe to grind, certainly none with the ability to make animals attack. Part of her job was hiring the right people for the right job, and no one worked for the zoo who didn't love animals and believe in their mission. There had been a dozen recent hires in the past six weeks, mostly in custodial staff and in anticipation of spring and summer—historically a busy time for the zoo. "Everyone loves zoo babies," Ms. Hartfield blithely added. The head of HR interlaced her fingers and placed them in her lap, an old trick she used to combat her nervous fidgeting—it wasn't every day the FBI wanted to speak to you. She had nothing to hide, but still felt like maybe she did. "I'm sorry I couldn't be more helpful."

Martinez took deep breath in and out to steady herself—there was a reason she hadn't gone into Human Resources. She plastered a reassuring smile on her face and fished out one of her FBI cards that redirected contacts to the Salt Mine. "Well, if you think of anything later or remember something that doesn't seem right in hindsight, please contact me."

It was hard to say who was more relieved: Ms. Hartfield to be rid of Martinez, or Martinez to be out of the head of HR's office. Martinez took the stairs to the third floor and came face-to-face with Melissa, Dr. Dumont's secretary.

"Agent Martinez," she exclaimed with surprise. "How was your meeting with Ms. Hartfield?"

"Fine," Martinez commented neutrally, "but I was hoping to have a quick word with Dr. Dumont."

Melissa's cheerful smile froze in place. "I'm afraid that's not possible. Dr. Dumont has a full schedule this morning." Martinez was all too accustomed to that tactic—her mother was the queen of "smile while you say no."

"If you could check—we will only take a minute of her time," Martinez politely insisted. She rode a fine line of intimating she had the full strength of the FBI behind her without actually having to produce any proof of said support.

Melissa punched buttons on her phone and spoke into her headset, "Dr. Dumont? Agent Martinez of the FBI is here requesting to see you for follow-up questions." Martinez couldn't hear the reply, but Melissa's pursed lips gave her a clue. "Certainly, Dr. Dumont," she answered deferentially. The secretary stood up and opened the door for Martinez. "Right this way, Agent Martinez."

"Good Morning, Agent Martinez," Dr. Dumont

summoned her to take a seat. "I understand you have a few more questions?"

"We believe we've found a possible link, if I may have a few minutes of your time," Martinez replied after the door had shut.

"As long as it's brief—I have another meeting, and need to leave in ten minutes."

Martinez withdrew a manila folder from her briefcase. "Could you take a look at this photo?"

Dr. Dumont's face lit up. "I haven't seen this picture in ages! It's hard to believe we were ever that young."

"So you recognize the people in the photo?"

"Sure—that's Cecila, Milo, me, and Steve. We were celebrating the new lab…must have been '93 or '94?"

"How were you acquainted with them?"

"We were all slogging through our graduate work at the same time. Celia and Milo were interested in exotic animals and conservation. Steve and I were more into animal behavior. But as you can see, we all shared the lab. You know the saying—misery loves company." Dr. Dumont glanced up from the picture with a curious look on her face. "What's all this about, Agent Martinez?"

"We have reason to believe your time together at OSU is at the heart of these animal attacks," Martinez evoked the royal we.

"That can't be! That was over twenty years ago," Dr.

Dumont dismissed the notion.

"Mr. Perkins is the owner of a petting zoo where a sheep attack occurred in January, and Ms. Marshall was killed in a zebra attack in February."

"Cecila's dead?" Her shock rang true to Martinez.

"I'm afraid so. You being the zoo director at the site of a third ungulate attack in almost as many months is simply too coincidental. You can understand the need to follow up on this. Do you have a last name for Steve?"

"Forester. It's Stephen Forester, with a 'ph'—he hated when people spelled his name wrong," Dr. Dumont spoke distantly, reciting a conversation from the ancient past. Martinez was tapping on her phone when Dr. Dumont suddenly asked, "Do you think Steve is behind these attacks?"

Martinez put her phone away. "What makes you ask that?"

Dr. Dumont, a pillar of polished poise yesterday, fumbled her words. "It's just…what happened all those years ago."

Martinez sat up and calmly spoke, "I think you'd better start from the beginning, Dr. Dumont."

The zoo director picked up her receiver and rang her secretary. "Melissa, please let Mr. Kinsey know that I will be late for our meeting. If necessary, reschedule for later." Then Charlotte Dumont poured herself a drink. "Would you like one?"

"No, thank you. But don't let that stop you," Martinez reassured her and waited for her tale to start.

"We were all scientists trying to make our mark—networking, trying to get on studies that were up and running, get our names on published papers…and with any luck, have our own research greenlighted and funded. We spent a lot of time in the library and the lab. It's fair to say we were all smart, but Steve was brilliant. He was always three or four steps ahead, making connections on things that were seemingly disparate." Dr. Dumont took a sip of amber liquid before continuing.

"As I said before, we shared a lab, and one day, the department called us in—there were discrepancies in lab supplies and equipment usage, and the department was concerned of resource misuse."

"Like theft?" Martinez speculated.

"Worse—conducting unauthorized research. No one at OSU does any experimentation on animals without clearance from IACUC, the Institutional Animal Care and Use Committee. It isn't concerned with the science per se, but how the animals are treated in the study; lots of protocols, and monitoring compliance with standards and regulatory requirements. It's a bureaucratic gauntlet and the bane of every researcher's existence—it's not uncommon to have to make multiple rounds of revisions before your study gets approved.

"During an unscheduled audit, it was discovered that disposable supplies and testing reagents were being consumed at a rapid rate, machine usage was well above logged time, and there were whispers among other researchers that their samples were either tampered with or missing. There was an internal review, and when it was all said and done, Steve was formally cautioned. He wasn't expelled or charged with any crimes, but even the implication of unethical activity was enough to sink his prospects."

"What do you mean?" Martinez asked.

Dr. Dumont finished the drink she had been nursing throughout her account. "Academia is a small pond—once you're blacklisted, it's over. No one wants you on their team. No one is going to write papers with you. No one is going to collaborate with you to bring more attention to your work. If you have a stain on your reputation, your work is considered tainted, regardless of the idea's merit. Even his advisor dropped him."

Dr. Dumont could tell by Martinez's face that she didn't understand the implications of such a move. "It's not uncommon for graduate students to use their masters as a time to solidify their focus and find an advisor who will guide them through to their PhD. Steve was hoping to continue his research at OSU with Dr. C as his primary advisor."

"Do you have a full name for Dr. C?" Martinez prompted Dumont.

"Everyone just called her Dr. C because her real name was ridiculous long and everyone mispronounced it. She was a tenured professor, Asian, somewhere in her mid-to-late 30s at the time," she grasped at straws sheepishly.

Martinez nodded sympathetically and guided Dumont forward—tracking down the name of a tenured professor should be a cakewalk for the analysts. "Back to the disciplinary action. What happened after that?"

She shrugged. "He wrapped up his graduate studies at OSU, applied for graduation, and was gone the next semester."

"Do you have any idea where he went or where he is now?"

"We didn't keep in touch—he thought one of us had sold him out."

Martinez knew she had to ask the question. "Did one of you?"

"I know I didn't," Dumont said defensively. "But I didn't speak on his behalf at the department-level hearing, either. None of us did. We were too afraid of suffering the same fate." She had a pained look on her face.

"It sounds like you had lost touch with Cecila and Milo as well?"

"We shared lab space and hung out occasionally, so it wasn't like we were the best of friends to start. But the entire ordeal put a strain on things. Milo and Cecila got their masters and moved on. I worked straight through to my doctorate and spent ten years in academia before going private sector. Until today, I hadn't thought of any of these people in years—it was another lifetime ago."

"Do you remember any of the other students or researchers that worked in the lab?"

Dumont shook her head. "I know there were other graduate students using the lab, but I can't recall any of their names. It was a long time ago," she answered apologetically.

"One more thing, and I'll leave you to your day. Do you remember Mr. Forester's field of interest?"

An enigmatic smile crept upon her face. "He flirted in molecular biology—in layman's terms, genetics. He did a little work on the genetic differences between African honeybees and European honeybees. This was the '90s—the human genome project was in full swing and everyone was hoping to find the gene responsible for everything—but what he focused on was the biologic underpinnings of aggression. He was interested in the cellular level—what was really happening when a grasshopper became a locust, a school of piranha became a feeding frenzy, or a betta fish saw another of its species and attacked."

Martinez withdrew another card and placed it on Dr. Dumont's desk. "If you think of something or remember anything, please contact me."

Chapter Nine

San Diego, California, USA
2nd of April, 1:00 p.m. (GMT-7)

Lukin finished his last pierogi, making sure to sop up the last dollop of sour cream and chopped herbs on the plate. He had become a regular diner at the Eastern European grocery store, whose three small round tables doubled as a cafe. It was a place where he could buy poppy seed rolls for breakfast, eat pierogis for lunch, and pick up snacks from home. Lukin wasn't one to question the Interior Council, but he hoped this scientist and his work was worth all this effort. The Ivory Tower agent had come close to declaring the mission a bust and requesting an abort—what was so impressive about a handful of nippy sheep and zebra kick in the head?—but once he saw the footage of the pronghorn attack, he knew it was mission critical. Antelopes are prey, and whatever caused prey to coordinate a hunt was exactly the kind of result the Interior Council wanted.

He was charged to follow Forester until his return to Ukraine, or until the Ivory Tower had a viable sample to derive the mechanism of the action. Lukin pulled out his mobile and tracked his package on its way out of San Diego. With any luck, he should be given permission to book a flight back to

Russia by the end of the week.

He flipped apps and watched Forester make his way east on I-40. Thankfully, the scientist hadn't switched rental cars yet, and Lukin's tracer was still in place. It had been hard going finding Forester at first; Lukin had arrived at the site of the first US attack with a name and a notion, unable to use the Tower's extensive information network as their reach did not cross the Atlantic. It wasn't until the second attack in New Mexico—Land of Enchantment...*da nyet!*—that Lukin got caught a break and picked up Forester's trail.

Since his arrival in North America, Forester hadn't boarded a plane, opting to drive everywhere and rarely more than six to eight hours a day. Lukin quickly gave up on the idea of following him by car, and opted to plant a tracker on Forester's rental instead. If the scientist stayed more than one night in a city, it was Lukin's signal to hop on a plane. Right now, Dr. Forester was on his way out of Albuquerque, and Lukin breathed a sigh of relief that he wasn't going to have to fly to New Mexico again.

Across the street, Wilson inconspicuously ate lunch on the patio, under the guise of making some vitamin D, where he could see if Lukin was meeting anyone over pierogis. Wilson deliberately gave Lukin a wide berth as to not alert him to his presence, but neither the tracker on Lukin's Ford nor the compass zeroed in on Lukin's magical signature was going to tell Wilson if the Russian was meeting someone, so he wanted to be eyes-on.

He lowered his gaze for a moment to his vibrating phone and read the text from Martinez. *L aka Peter Melkin, USA. Travel and CC dig started.*

Wilson briefly entertained the notion of picking up Lukin on a phony passport and neutralizing him once and for all, but that would have been ultimately counterproductive to the current mission, not to mention the sheer magnitude of ire Leader would rain down on him if he chose to escalate the situation. No, if he was going to take out Lukin, Leader would want it to occur outside of the US and have the appearance of either self-defense or operational casualty. Another phone vibration brought him out of his ruminations.

Martinez: *To hospital - E is awake. SM sent Forester pic.* Wilson opened the attachment and studied the doughy man in his late forties, with sand-colored side-swept hair and a bland smile that didn't reach his humorless dark brown eyes. Dressed in a buttoned-down shirt and blazer, it looked like the adult equivalent of a school picture, something to tote out for conference brochures and official websites.

Thx. Happy hunting, he replied and sipped his Arnold Palmer.

*****

Martinez navigated her way around Scripps Mercy Hospital

with ease. She had spent plenty of time in hospitals of all sizes over the years, and they generally had a similar floor plan once you got on the unit. The cardinal rule of hospitals? When in doubt, find the nurses' station. After a few introductions with her badge and ID, Martinez located Marco Estevez's room on a med-surge unit.

The door was open, so Martinez knocked on the wall outside before entering. "Mr. Estevez?" she called out.

"In here," a voice hollered. Martinez crossed the threshold, and the medicinal smell of antiseptic filled her nostrils. Somewhere in his mid-thirties, Marco Estevez was awake and sitting up in bed, dressed in a hospital gown with an abdominal binder snuggly wrapped around his middle. He had an IV line in his left arm, and the button for timed pain medication wasn't far from his hand. Everything he could need was within arm's reach: a jug of water with a straw, a bedside urinal hooked to the side of the bed, an extra pillow, tissues, and the call button.

"I am Special Agent Martinez from the FBI. I'm here to speak to a Marco Estevez." She flashed her badge and identification one more time. He managed to muster a smile despite the cuts and contusions on his face and the obvious pain he was in.

"Whatever happened, I didn't do it. I've been in the hospital all weekend—just ask the nurses," he joked.

Martinez let out a small smile. "I believe you. I saw the videos of the attack. You're lucky to be alive."

"So everyone keeps telling me, but they aren't the ones stuck in the hospital and not allowed to eat real food," he observed wryly. "But I'm sure you didn't come here to hear me grouse or to smuggle me a burger. What can I do for you, Special Agent Martinez? Please tell me it's the burger thing."

"I'm investigating the attack at the zoo last weekend, and I would like to ask you a few questions, if you feel up to it," she stated respectfully.

"I'm all yours."

"I understand you are responsible for the day-to-day care of the camels and the pronghorns, is that correct?"

"And a few other exhibits…but yes, that's correct."

"In the days preceding the incident, was there anything out of the ordinary—a break in routine, an unscheduled visitor, anything unusual about the animals?"

His brow furrowed in concentration, but after a moment, he shrugged with a slight wince. "Not that I can think of. It was business as usual."

"We think someone may have tampered with the animals. I would like you to take a look at a few pictures." She pulled out a folder and produced blown-up pictures of Lukin and Forester. Do you recognize either of these men?"

He studied Lukin's photo and shook his head before moving onto the next photo. After a long pause, Estevez spoke, "He looks different in the picture, but I think that's the new delivery guy."

"Different how?" Martinez started taking notes.

"Well, he wasn't wearing a suit for one," Estevez quipped, "and he's thinner. But the face is the same."

"Do you remember when he started coming to the zoo?"

"He came last week with our typical shipment—said the normal driver was out sick."

"And who is the normal driver?"

"Don't know his last name, but his nametag said 'Joe.'"

"Back to him." Martinez tapped the picture with her finger. "Did he have any contact with the animals?"

"Nope, just brought the feed and the salt blocks and left."

Martinez mulled over this new information. "Is that something both the camels and the pronghorns use?"

"The feed, yes, but we don't give the camels salt blocks. Their tongues are too short to lick them so they end up biting them—it's bad for their teeth," he stated knowingly. He was a zookeeper through and through, even hooked up to tubes in the hospital.

"Do you remember which day that was?"

"We always get the feed delivery on Wednesdays unless we special order something," he answered confidently.

Martinez finished her notes, retrieved the photos, and pulled out another card. "Thank you for your help, Mr. Estevez. If you remember anything else, please contact me. I hope you have a speedy recovery."

*****

Lukin pulled out his earbuds and swore. *Why are the FBI poking around?* He'd assumed state agencies would investigate, but federal interest implied another level of complication. It meant that someone had made a connection between the San Diego animal attack and at least one other attack. And this was the second time he had heard of Agent Martinez in the past twenty-four hours; he didn't like how often she was appearing in the middle of his mission. Were he not in North America, he could use his contacts to find out more information or stymie the investigation until the Ivory Tower had what it wanted. Lukin was kicking himself for only planting a listening device in Estevez's room—if only he could have gotten a look at those photos and seen who they deemed as persons of interest. He brooded over his coffee, considering his next course of action.

Chapter Ten

The obsidian blue pearl Honda CR-V pulled up to the craftsman bungalow nestled in a cul-de-sac in Edmond, one of the up-and-coming suburbs just north of Oklahoma City. The driver nervously fished out a worn envelope and checked the address against the metallic numbers affixed to the house—it was a match. He couldn't be certain she still lived here, it was the last known address he had for her, stamped on a four-year-old Christmas card.

He surveyed himself in the mirror, straightening his dark blond hair and shirt. Most of yesterday evening had been dedicated to meticulously putting his best foot forward, included a stop at the barbers. Not only did he get a haircut, the barber tamed his wily eyebrows and trimmed his ear and nose hair. Then, there was the inordinate amount of time spent on what he should wear; he generally subscribed to the notion that it was better to dress up than down, but it seemed wrong to wear a suit to visit your daughter—not to mention how baggy his suit had become over the past three months. In the end, he had laid out a collared buttoned-down shirt and khakis but kept his formal shoes, which he'd polished to a shine before bed.

As usual, he didn't have much of an appetite first thing in the morning, but he knew the nausea would be worse if he ate nothing. He had choked down a plain bagel with a little peanut butter before he'd left, and made sure he had plenty of pills in case the nausea hit him on the road.

He cut the engine and climbed out of the driver's seat. His hard-bottomed shoes fell crisp on the bluestone pavers that led to the front porch painted blue, gray, and white. It was quaint, with an American flag hoisted in a metal notch and a naturally finished cedar gliding bench.

Stephen Forester was pretty sure this was a bad idea, but he was running out of time to make things perfect—it was either good enough or not at all. He reached for the doorbell and heard the chimes through the door. The rapid patter of flat-footed steps approached before a three-foot-tall girl opened the front door. "Hi!" she greeted Forester, slightly breathless from running. Blonde feathery wisps that had escaped her braid fluttered around her face.

Forester bent down to speak to her eye-to-eye, "Is your mommy home?"

Without answering him, the girl turned back into the house and yelled, "Mommy, it's for you!"

From around a curve, a peeved voice sounded. "Maddy,

what did I tell you about answering the door? Only Daddy and I do that." Jane turned the corner, wiping her hands on a red-and-white-checkered kitchen towel. Dressed in faded jeans and a pale blue sweater with little to no makeup and her hair in a ponytail, she looked more like a teenager than a mom. Her brown eyes rose from her daughter, and she came face-to-face with Stephen Forester and froze. Even Maddy could sense something was happening as Jane stopped breathing for a split second.

Forester rose to his full height before greeting her. "Hi, Janey." His voice broke the spell.

Jane tore her eyes from the door and placed herself between Forester and her daughter. "Maddy, why don't you go to your room and play," she suggested in a high register and a buoyant tone.

"But Mommy—" the girl began.

Jane summoned her mom voice, "Now." Maddy knew her mom was serious when she used that voice and sulked her way further into the house. Jane waited until she heard Maddy's heavy tread in her room upstairs before addressing her unexpected visitor. "What are you doing here?!" It came out half question and half accusation.

"I'm in the US for work and was passing through Oklahoma City," he fibbed. "I wasn't sure if you were still at this address, but I thought I'd stop by and try."

Jane had one hand on the frame and another on the door

itself, creating a wall across the entrance to the house. "Well, I'm still here. What do you want?"

He looked for traces of the little girl he remembered in the grown woman that barricaded the door. She looked so much like her mother, but she had his nose. "I just wanted to see you and how you were doing," he replied weakly. "It looks like you are doing well for yourself."

"Yeah, things are good," she responded tersely. "This was fun; maybe we'll do this again in another twenty years." She stepped back to close the door but Forester shoved his foot and arm inside.

"Wait! Could I meet Maddy?" he pleaded.

"You already have," she insisted.

"But she doesn't know I'm her grandfather."

Jane leveled her eyes and voice, "She already has a grandfather—his name is Dennis. He was there at her birth. He has either been present for or video-called her on every birthday and holiday Hallmark makes a card for. He also walked me down the aisle at my wedding and showed up for every game, recital, and ceremony you missed. So Maddy's good. I'm good. Please remove yourself from my doorway," she firmly requested.

Forester started to sweat—this was going sideways fast. "I'm sorry things ended up like this, Janey. I won't bother you again." He removed himself from the doorway and turned to leave.

"You wanna know why I stopped sending Christmas cards?" Her pointed question stopped his retreat.

He turned around. At least she's still talking to me. "Why?"

"For years, I kept making excuses for you. You are really dedicated to your work and your research was important—that's why you left for Ukraine. But once I had Maddy, I finally got it. It wasn't important; it was *more* important to you than your family. That was your choice. When I became a parent, I finally figured out that I wasn't the problem.

"So I don't know what brought you here and I don't really care, but don't pretend that it's because you care about me. Whatever is going on, it's about you because it's *always* been about you." With that, Jane closed the door and locked it.

Stephen Forester got into his rental car and drove away. The hopeful part of him had thought about leaving his things at the hotel on the off chance things went well and he would need more time in Oklahoma City, but caution prompted him to pack everything before he came—the last thing he needed was to lose the last of the serum before he had finished his work. He pulled into a gas station, and a wave of nausea took hold as he replayed the encounter. He popped a dissolvable tablet under his tongue and waited for the medication to kick in. He didn't blame Janey for being upset—it wasn't her fault; it was theirs. A well of anger roiled from deep within, overwhelming the nausea. The automatic shutoff on the gas pump clicked, bringing him back to the here and now.

What's done is done, he told himself as he withdrew the pump and screwed on the gas tank cap. He had nothing left to do but this one last coda. He slid into the driver's seat once more, and the Honda CR-V roared back to life. Shifting the car into drive, Stephen Forester turned on his signal before merging into traffic heading northeast on I-44.

Chapter Eleven

San Diego, California, USA
3rd of April, 10:00 a.m. (GMT-7)

Lukin gloved up and wiped everything down in his hotel room. He would have loved to have torched the place, but that would have been less than discreet, and the last thing he wanted was to attract attention. If Forester was done with San Diego, than so was Lukin, especially if federal agents were investigating.

If given his druthers, Lukin would have waited until Forester had stopped at his next destination before flying out, but he had not lived long enough to be a senior Ivory Tower agent without cause. He had two more American passports; it was time to burn Peter Melkin.

Erring on the side of caution, Lukin operated under the assumption that he was under some form of surveillance and took care to appear business as usual. Last night, he'd set everything in place for his charade; now it was show time. He picked up his small suitcase and left Room 312 for the last time.

Sliding the luggage into the back seat, Lukin visually swept the parking lot. Unsurprisingly, he recognized many of the cars, but that wasn't what he was looking for. He was looking for people inside parked cars; not many people book a hotel room to stay in their car, and only a tail would be sitting in their car this early in the morning. Finding nothing untoward, Lukin took to the driver's seat and drove the Ford Fiesta to the rental car return at San Diego International Airport, flicking his eyes to the rearview mirror at regular intervals. The attendant took the keys, noted the mileage, and handed Lukin a printed receipt of return.

He aped the other commuters waiting for the airport shuttle, fiddling with his phone while keeping a firm hand on his baggage and eyes active, scanning the nearby area. He made sure to be first on the shuttle so he could take a seat in the back, giving him unfettered views of the other passengers as they entered: a couple traveling with two young children, three business travelers, and two women in their 20s traveling together. The ten-minute shuttle stopped first at terminal one before moving to the larger terminal two. Lukin exited last and checked in Peter Melkin for his flight to Seattle, Washington.

He cleared security, boarding pass and ID in hand. Once on the other side, he performed the travel song and dance, getting food and taking a seat to wait for a flight, but he covertly left Peter Melkin's credit card on a public bench—he wouldn't be needing it anymore, and if anyone was using it to track his movements, it would be another form of misinformation in his favor. Lukin didn't have enough faith in humanity to believe that whoever found it wouldn't try to use it at least once.

Wheeling his suitcase into a bathroom stall, he began the next phase of his escape out of San Diego. First, he changed his clothing, donned glasses, and converted the case into a backpack. Next, he wove a spell he called *the kaleidoscope* upon himself—as long as he held the spell in his mind, everyone that saw him would see a different version of him. It wouldn't fool the cameras, but if asked, no two people would give the same description of the Russian—one might say he was a short mustachioed man wearing glasses with black hair and brown eyes, while the person next to them would say he was in fact a tall portly man with white hair and an unfortunate goatee. And if anyone was canvassing the area, neither could peg him as the man in the photo.

Lukin left the bathroom and exited the terminal through baggage claim. Following the signs, he hailed a taxi. The cab driver was initially unwilling to take the man to Los Angeles International Airport, but when Lukin offered to pay cash up front, he agreed. Once they were on the highway leading away from the San Diego airport, Lukin let his spell drop. He had every intention of wiping the cabbie's memory of this escapade once they arrived at LAX, and there was no need to spend more magic. He was already noticing some potential karmic backlash—he was not a clumsy man, and his collection of stubbed toes, jammed fingers, and other assorted minor injuries had prompted him to make a donation to an animal shelter the other day.

According to Lukin's reckoning, it would take two to three hours by car, depending on how atrocious traffic was. Lukin took off his glasses and changed his shirt. His backpack became a suitcase again, this time with a removable sticker indicating affiliation with a sports team. After a few rebuffed attempts at conversation, the driver took Lukin's hint and turned up the music to fill the silence.

A few hours later, the taxi pulled to the drop-off curb, and Lukin cast his incantation on his way out. The taxi driver blinked back to reality as the car behind him blared its horn. He pulled out of the way to let the car pass, but he couldn't work out why his taxi was sitting outside LAX. He had the same confusion when he finally got home and emptied his pockets to find $600 in folded bills.

Once inside, Lukin purchased a ticket under a new alias for a direct flight to Oklahoma City, the last city in which Forester had stayed overnight. Navigating LAX was a nightmare like always, but Lukin took solace that it was the last place the FBI would be looking for him. He took a seat at his gate and checked his watch—they would be making final boarding calls for Peter Melkin any moment now.

*****

After following up on a few more leads at the zoo and with its suppliers, Martinez grabbed an early dinner and retreated to her hotel room to put the pieces of the puzzle together. All things considered, she'd had a productive day. Dr. Dumont had sent her a copy of the lab results from UCLA—no *rabies lyssavirus* detected in brain tissue under immunofluorescent staining on microscopic examination, no rabies lyssavirus in culture. The zoo director had managed to pull a few more names from her memory, including the full name of Dr. C: Camille Chevapravatdumrong. Martinez had put a priority on tracking Peter Melkin and Stephen Forester yesterday, but now that she had Forester's file, the Salt Mine would be able to cross-reference the names and check for zoo or animal affiliations in anticipation of another attack.

Armed with Forester's photo, Martinez had canvassed the other zoo staff—who recognized him as last week's deliveryman—and the security video confirmed that he arrived in the supplier's van and left after making his drop-off. It didn't definitively disprove direct contact with the pronghorns preceding the attack, but made it unlikely. The feed was used in both the camel and pronghorn enclosures, but the salt delivered to Estevez was used exclusively by the pronghorns. Even though the salt blocks were delivered on Wednesday, they weren't put out until Saturday morning—used to encourage the animals out from their privacy shelters into the open for visitor viewing. Martinez would have taken the remains of the blocks for testing if they hadn't already been destroyed per zoo protocol.

Then she had paid a visit to the zoo's supplier, SoCal Feed and Animal Supplies. She had tracked down the normal delivery driver, a Mr. Joseph Cooper, who had worked the day Forester delivered to the zoo but reported he was pulled from his normal route to deliver a rush job out of town. When questioned, the manager hadn't recalled making the request; however, he readily admitted that his primary concern was that everything got delivered and all the trucks came back to the lot before the gates closed. There was no log of when trucks came and went throughout the workday; the only records they kept were proof-of-delivery and odometer readings taken at the beginning and end of each day. Forester's picture had also been a bust; no one could positively identify him as one of the drivers on the day in question, but the manager didn't recognize him as someone he had hired recently.

Martinez stashed her to-go cheesecake in the hotel mini-fridge and changed before turning her attention to Stephen Forester's file. Stephen Elliot Forester, age 49, born in Pataskala, OH; spent the first thirty years of his life within a hundred miles of his birthplace before leaving for Ukraine. He'd been married once, divorced shortly after leaving the country, and his ex-wife won full custody of their only child. A few years later, he obtained his PhD at the Institute of Molecular Biology and Genetics of the National Academy of Sciences of Ukraine, where he was currently listed as a department head—which made getting a hold of a current picture significantly easier, since he didn't have a presence on social media.

A year ago, he renewed his US passport at the US Embassy in Kiev, using the same permanent address listed on his US tax forms, and re-entered America at DFW with an immediate connection to Las Vegas shortly before Christmas—two weeks before the first animal attack. There were no flight records within the US after that, but there were a series of charges from a car rental company on his credit card history, the repeated amounts indicating a weekly renewal. Charges on the same card confirmed Forester was in the general area up to ten days before all three attacks, as well as a series of purchases at feed and supply stores when he got into town. The Salt Mine was working on requesting more information from the rental car company, but a series of charges at gas stations and hotels pegged Forester as making his way east with his last fill-up on I-44, just northeast of Oklahoma City.

Martinez bit her lip as she pondered—it wasn't hard to make your own salt licks; her dad use to make a mineral lick to attract deer. After a quick web search on animals that use salt or mineral licks, she found a prevalence of ungulates on the list, including sheep, zebras, and pronghorns. *Whatever Forester is giving the animals, he's doing it through the salt*, she thought to herself. It was unlikely to be supernatural—salt neutralized magic, and was used to safely pack and transport magical items.

So what the hell is he giving them? She scrolled through a series of articles and conference brochures the analysts had dug up online.

Martinez was impressed by the amount of information they'd found in twenty-four hours, and it confirmed her belief that the internet was like how you treat your biggest bag— you never bothered to tidy it until it was absolutely stuffed, except there was no limit to how much crap you could cram into the web. As long as the server storing the information was still running, there was an endless amount of minutia for download, including a conference brochure from five years ago and that published article written seven years ago.

Martinez started up the coffee maker and did a deep dive. He was still interested in animal aggression, and did his PhD on biomarkers as "the intermediate to phenotypic expression of aggression." As far as she could work out, Forester collaborated across different departments—when it was his specialty, he got first billing, otherwise he would be listed as a secondary author. With judicious use of the internet to fill in the gaps on jargon, Martinez flipped through his published works—reading the summations, skipping over the data and statistical analyses, and picking up the conclusions at the end. She felt like she was back in college taking her obligatory science classes.

After bringing herself up to speed with his publications, she changed gears and reviewed his professional appearances. In the past ten years, Forester's name frequently showed up as a panelist at molecular biology conferences in Europe and Asia involving metabolomics and epigenetics. Martinez consulted the hive mind that was the internet once again.

Metabolomics: the scientific study of the set of metabolites present within an organism, cell, or tissue.

Epigenetics: the study of changes in organisms caused by modification of gene expression rather than alteration of the genetic code itself.

Tiring, she stretched her legs and did some calisthenics to get her blood pumping, and then dove back in, trying to pull together threads to weave them into something comprehensible. Biology 101: everything in the body comes down to proteins, and DNA is essentially a giant book of recipes for proteins— she recalled that much from her last biology class almost ten years ago.

It was thought that genes simply determined what would happen in an individual—you have Gene A, you have blue eyes; you have Gene B, you have brown hair—but after they finished sequencing the human genome, they discovered that most of the genetic material in DNA was *not* protein recipes. At first, it was regarded as filler—the genetic equivalent of white noise—but as more research occurred, it was thought to have a purpose. For example, the ends of chromosomes called telomeres were protective, making sure the bits clipped off during replication were junk instead of valuable genetic information.

As for the inscrutable parts in the middle of a string of DNA, scientists thought they were parameters on when a cell was supposed to make a particular protein—a genetic on-off switch. A distant memory wiggled deep in Martinez's brain from the time she went to the genetic counselor with her mother when they found out breast cancer ran in their family. The counselor had referred to it as "genetic predisposition." Just because you have a particular gene doesn't mean the gene will be expressed, and other factors affect whether or not that gene is activated. Martinez felt like she was on a roll and hurried to her laptop to get her ruminations down before she lost her train of thought.

She then scrolled back over her notes from her interview with Dr. Dumont, the only person with a PhD in biology that she had spoken to in the course of investigating Forester. *Forester wanted to know what was going on when a grasshopper turned into a locust.* That sentence resonated with Martinez in light of all his recent articles. There were plenty of short-horned grasshoppers that remained solitary grasshoppers; what was going on inside the grasshopper that morphed into a gregarious feeding machine? What gene or genes was it turning on or off? Somewhere between "hormones, neurotransmitters, and inflammation biomarkers" was the underlying biology of aggression that Forester dedicated decades of his life to understanding. Was it possible that he found a way to flip the switch?

Her phone beeped and broke her concentration; it was a text from Wilson. *We have a problem - L gone.*

Chapter Twelve

Stephen Forester barreled east, taking the loop around Indianapolis to avoid city traffic. He knew he was getting close to Ohio when he saw the signs for Skyline Chili and couldn't resist. He preemptively placed another dissolvable tablet under his tongue and managed to eat a 4-Way with onions. Nowhere else in the world could one find chili served on spaghetti.

He had intentionally saved Columbus for last, in part because he was ambivalent about returning to his roots. Ohio was the place where everything good began—where he grew up, found his passion for biology, fell in love, and married Kelly, who made him a home that became complete with Janey's birth. But it was also where everything fell apart—his research ended, his career stymied, his marriage broken, his home in ruins.

He knew Janey blamed him for leaving, but it was over long before he boarded that plane with two suitcases. She made it sound like he didn't try, but he did. She was just too young to remember. He tried working private sector—in labs, industrial manufacturing, oil and coal, pharmaceuticals—wherever his Masters of Science could open doors. And it would be fine for a while, until he got bored. Until he figured out how things worked better than his bosses. Until he felt trapped in a life not of his choosing.

He was drowning, and on a lark, he applied to do his doctorate at the Institute of Molecular Biology and Genetics of the National Academy of Sciences of Ukraine. It was a self-governing state-funded organization that was flourishing in its post-Soviet freedoms. They attracted scientists and researchers from all over the world, and the shadow that followed him in the provincial pool of academia among North American universities did not darken his prospects in Eastern Europe. They even had an English journal where he could publish his research. He could start again, and he'd had every intention of bringing Kelly and Janey with him. He kept telling himself that he would go and check things out, and that his family would come when called.

It was easy to see all the signs in hindsight. How many times did he accuse Kelly of not being supportive, instead of listening to the numerous ways she was trying to tell him she didn't want to uproot their lives? How many times did he see everything she'd built as a weight dragging him down? How many nights and weekends did Janey spend at her grandparents because Kelly didn't want her to see them fighting again? If he had been a wiser man, he would have understood that they were already slipping away and taking that flight to Europe was the nail in the coffin. It was only because of his hubris that he was surprised when he received the divorce papers in the mail. But God help him, he would do it all over again, in spite of everything.

In time, he'd become accustomed to life in Kiev and even picked up conversational Ukrainian, but it had never felt like home. No matter how routine things became, it still wasn't right in some fundamental way…like a persistent irritation crawling just under the surface of his skin.

He hadn't been sure how he was going to feel when he returned to Ohio, and he was relieved when an eerie calm came over him as the Honda passed under the "Welcome to Ohio" sign. He knew that, however imperfect the circumstance, he had finally come home. He'd had to leave to do his work, but he refused to die in exile.

Once he passed the sign, the white-on-green countdown began— first to Dayton and then to Columbus, the state capital and home to Ohio State University's main campus. *We are all counting down*, he bleakly joked to himself.

Forester was a private man, who kept to himself. There wasn't anyone in Kiev with whom he'd felt the need to share his diagnosis, and he certainly didn't tell anyone at work. Not only was it none of their business, it would have been a distraction from all the irons he had in the fire. By the time the doctors caught it, it had already spread. He had considered radiation and chemo; as a scientist, he had access to the most recent research and could do all the math to figure the statistical probabilities of eradication or remission. But there was no way for him to account for the non-numerical factors until he found himself considering those three fateful words: quality of life.

Had his research been approved, he would have stayed until his condition prevented him from working. He'd had wonderful success with Serum 132 in his mice study. He had effectively convinced cells that they were in a state of oxidative stress without actually harming them, so much so that it changed their genetic expression toward aggression—their serotonergic activity plummeted and they became rabid. Forester applied for further research, but where he saw progress, the review board saw "cruel treatment of animals with minimal scientific benefit."

The rejection on ethical grounds tore open an old wound he had long considered healed. Facing mortality gave him a moment of clarity—it all started at OSU with the disciplinary hearing. If things had gone right there, the rest of his life would have had a very different trajectory.

His rejection had been infuriating, so he'd privately made tweaks to the serum to translate it to ungulates and discreetly conducted small proof-of-concept tests while still working at the Institute. Once the new formula had been adjusted to take into account the difference in physiology and neurobiology, Forester had produced more serum; enough to fulfill the needs of his North American trip.

His colleagues had been surprised at his decision to take a sabbatical, considering his history of continuous toil, but they could not begrudge him the time off. They felt it was healthy for academics to take a break from their work from time to time. Little did they know that Dr. Stephen Forester had no intention of returning to either the Institute or Ukraine. They also were unaware of the illicit vials of modified Serum 132 tucked into Forester's attaché on his last day at the lab. In a fit of spite, Forester even removed all his papers and wiped his computer, assuring they could not piggyback off any of his innovations once he was gone.

The gas light lit up on his dashboard, breaking his reminiscing—he had forgotten to fill up after the 4-Way! He cursed and started looking for the nearest gas station. He had anticipated the progressive physical symptoms—the fatigue, nausea, loss of appetite, weight loss—but those things didn't bother him nearly as much as the cognitive changes. He was a man of the mind, and the diminished concentration and mental fog were by far the greater insult to him. Forester turned on his signal and steered the Honda into the exit lane.

Chapter Thirteen

Columbus, Ohio, USA
4th of April, 7:00 p.m. (GMT-4)

Davis Watson left San Diego and reemerged as Special Agent Wilson of the FBI in Columbus, OH. Despite the optics of dining al fresco in polo shirts and shades, Wilson felt good returning to a suit and clean shave—he wasn't really on vacation, and it felt a little off working in casual attire.

He was still peeved that Lukin had slipped through his fingers, but he had enough operation discipline to keep his focus on the objective. The constructed timeline of Forester's and Peter Melkin's movements over the past few months indicated that Lukin was following the attacks and eventually Forester. The Ivory Tower wanted something from the scientist, so as long as he and Martinez ruled out the supernatural and secured Forester, mission accomplished.

After the analysts discovered that Dr. Chevapravatdumrong was made a professor emerita at OSU a few years ago—akin to a retirement position—and spent much of her time volunteering at the Columbus Zoo and Aquarium, they booked a flight to Ohio. The Salt Mine had filed the appropriate requests while he and Martinez were in midair, and they now had a license plate and remote access to the GPS in Forester's rented Honda CR-V.

They booked adjoining rooms at the hotel across the street from the place Forester was staying—they could see his motel room door from Martinez's window. Wilson took first watch through the binoculars while Martinez combed through the data set from the GPS. "Most of his stops are gas, food, hotels, and supply stores," Martinez observed aloud. "He hits the pharmacies pretty regularly, too, every couple of weeks." She checked a few of the addresses on the web. "Looks like he visits stores with walk-in clinics inside."

"Cheaper and faster than the emergency room," Wilson noted.

"Huh." She paused, tapping an address into her search engine. "He made a residential stop in Oklahoma." She pulled up the street view; it was so heartland America, it was almost a self-parody. "A quaint craftsman with a front porch flying an American flag."

Wilson noted the touch of sarcasm in her voice. "Maybe he visited a friend or some family?" he offered a guess, keeping his sights on the blue Honda, waiting for it to leave so they could get a look at Forester's room. "Guy hasn't been back to the US in decades."

"Who makes social visits between bioterrorism destinations?" she asked rhetorically. Martinez logged into the

FBI database and did a quick search. "Co-owned by Mark and Jane Kranton."

"Isn't his daughter's name Jane?" Wilson offered as he saw Forester's door open. "We've got movement."

Martinez looked up but stayed seated—this wasn't her first stakeout. "Is he leaving or just refilling the ice bucket?"

"He just fired up his car," Wilson reported. Martinez secured her devices and geared up.

It was still light out, but rainclouds that had been sputtering rain all afternoon, and the darkened skies and weather provided a modicum of cover—everyone was going about their business for fear of being caught in the rain. Wilson and Martinez took their chances—Forester hadn't left the room since he'd checked in, and there was no telling how long he would be gone.

They drove across the street—Columbus wasn't a pedestrian city apart from the OSU campus, and going by foot would have made them conspicuous—and parked in an open space around the corner from Forester's room. The drizzle gave them the perfect excuse to obscure their features—heads buried under umbrellas, clothing smothered in jackets, and gloves to conceal their prints. Any parking lot camera would have captured two indistinct people running to their room to escape the rain. Wilson had his phone ready, using an application Weber installed that worked as a skeleton key for electronic door systems. Once the green light flashed on the panel, Wilson opened the door, letting Martinez enter first and collapsing his umbrella only after they were both inside.

Forester had closed the curtain before he left, and the room was pitch-black with the door shut. They both turned on their flashlights and surveyed their surroundings. It was a standard motel room: two queen beds with two nightstands, a mini-fridge with microwave on top next to a circular table with two chairs that could be a makeshift desk or dining area, a nook with a luggage rack where Forester's suitcase rested, a tiled area with a sink outside of the bathroom itself, and a full-length mirror attached to some random patch of wall.

The table was covered with loose salt, as was much of the carpet where an empty sack of fine stock salt lay. The wastebasket held empty containers of molasses and a handful of empty unmarked three-ounce bottles—the kind drug stores sell travelers to get their shampoo and body gel through TSA. Whatever Forester was cooking up, he had failed to clean the kitchen before he left.

Martinez checked the drawers while Wilson started blowing salt— the place was already covered in granules, so he felt no need to obfuscate his magical sweep. While Wilson waited for magical signatures, Martinez found prescription bottles and took pictures of them with her phone. Next, she opened his luggage and carefully searched, making note of where everything was when she first opened it. She found nothing untoward or hidden in the suitcase itself, but did notice the luggage rack poked out of the closet a few inches.

Martinez waved her beam behind the folding rack and spotted four two-liter bottles, stripped of their labels and placed against the wall. Whatever drink that once filled them was gone; instead, they were filled three-quarters full of salt. A dark viscous fluid filled the top of the bottles, creating a stark demarcation where the salt ended and the molasses began. She readied her vape pen and dispersed the fine salt with her breath, fixing her light on the area. "I think I found the next batch of killer salt," she announced, "but it's not magic."

Wilson poked his head out from the bathroom he had just salted. "There's nothing magical here." Despite his proclamation, he pulled out a plastic bag and collected some hair from the comb on the counter…just in case. He checked his watch—they had cleared the room in less than ten minutes. They gathered their things and wiped down the tile to remove any shoeprints that would alert Forester to their visit.

Martinez and Wilson made their exit and agreed to grab some takeout before heading back to their hotel. Martinez broke into her piping hot fries as soon as Wilson handed her the bag—she gave herself a dispensation from healthy eating while traveling. "So, what's our next move?" she asked between clenched teeth and short breaths, trying to cool down the mash of potato that had just come out of the fryer.

Wilson kept his eyes on the road. "Pass along what we have to the local FBI branch, and move on."

Martinez glared at him. "That's it? It's our case, and there are still so many unanswered questions."

"And the next agents assigned to this case will be the ones tasked to find those answers," he replied matter-of-factly. "Our part is done. Lukin failed to obtain the blood samples and has fallen off our radar. Whatever Forester is doing is not magical. With the evidence we have, he'll be in custody soon enough and no longer a threat." Wilson pulled into a parking space and turned off the engine. "You're Salt Mine now, Martinez, not FBI."

"But he's a bad guy we've been chasing. Don't you want to be the one to get him?" she countered.

"This time tomorrow, we'll be home getting ready for the weekend, and Forester will be someone else's concern. Case closed."

Chapter Fourteen

Columbus, Ohio, USA
5th of April, 8:30 a.m. (GMT-4)

Agent Kyle Rogers scurried out of the elevator and toward his desk, hoping no one had noticed he was late—he had plans tonight and he really didn't want to stay late to finish out his workweek. Agent Jeremy Lee looked up from his monitor long enough to give Rogers a look of mild disapproval. "You're late," Lee stated neutrally. "Again."

"Maybe I'm just thirty minutes early for a nine to five?" Rogers charismatically suggested as he grabbed his mug and loaded it up with free office coffee; he hadn't time this morning to hit North Market for his favorite brew and giant cinnamon bun.

Lee scoffed at the notion. "The day you don't cut out early on a Friday afternoon is the day I grow wings and fly away."

"Hey buddy, don't be so hard on yourself. I know you've put on a few pounds over the years, but don't call yourself a pig. It's not fair to the pigs," he ribbed his partner of three years. Lee did not deign to give a response and returned to his paperwork. Rogers fired up his computer and put his things away before turning his attention to his cup. The coffee was palpable, thanks to the heaping scoops of sugar and a healthy shot of flavored creamer purloined from the fridge. "What's going on in Fischer's office?" He nodded to the special agent's closed door. Even the blinds where shut.

"Beats me—it was like that when I got here this morning. At eight," Lee clarified for emphasis. He continued typing, putting the final touches on his report before he could put their most recent case to bed. "And done!" he announced triumphantly. "Next time, you're doing the paperwork."

"But you're so much better at it than I am," Rogers pointed out with a generous dose of flattery.

"True, but it would be a shame if Fischer were to find out why our last car was defaced." Lee rose to collect his report from the office printer.

The young agent sighed with resignation. "You make a compelling argument." Rogers picked up a file on his desk and took a circuitous route to the copier that had him pass close to Fischer's door. He paused for a few seconds—bent down to retie his shoelaces—and tilted an ear toward the door. All he could hear were muffled voices: Fischer's, another man, and a woman. He heard chairs scraping against the floor and hustled back to his desk.

The Federal Bureau of Investigations' resident agency in Columbus, Ohio was situated in the heart of the arena district, not far from downtown, German Village, and the

Short North. Its headquarters were located inside one of the many nondescript brick-faced office buildings that littered the corporate-suburban landscape. Covering the counties of Delaware, Fairfield, Fayette, Franklin, Knox, Licking, Madison, Morrow, Pickaway, and Union, Agents Rogers and Lee spent most of their time looking into tips, investigating cases filtered through the Cincinnati Regional Field Office, or acting as local support in larger investigations spearheaded by more senior agents. Led by Special Agent James Fischer, their operation was busy, but routine, which made visitors behind closed doors all the more intriguing.

All morning patter ceased when Fischer's office door opened abruptly. Rogers and Lee did their best to conceal their curiosity in business as usual when the two guests emerged from their supervisor's domain. Their demeanor and inoffensively sober clothing said g-men, even if one of them was a very striking woman—what Rogers's granddad would euphemistically refer to as "a tall drink of water." Lee—who had an eye, but not the budget, for the finer things in life—noted the male agent's suit, shoes, and attaché; whoever he was, he was way above Lee's pay grade. After they strode through the office and took the stairs down, Special Agent James Fischer unbuttoned his jacket and let out his breath. "Rogers, Lee—in my office," he ordered.

Rogers gestured for Lee to enter first. "Age before beauty," he snidely quipped.

"Just get in here. And don't kid yourself—neither of you

are much to look at," Fischer barked as he took his jacket off and closed the file on his desk—he had already flipped through it as Special Agents Martinez and Wilson briefed him. It wasn't unusual for cases to get reassigned in the bureau, but the circumstances seemed odd to the seasoned federal agent. In his experience, reassignment happened when something prohibited the agents from work, they weren't getting anywhere on the case, or the case moved higher up the food chain and required heavier guns. Most of the time, agents *wanted* to stay on their cases and were merely requesting additional resources at local FBI offices, but Special Agents Martinez and Wilson were all too happy to give up their investigation and move on to their next case.

From where Fischer sat, much of the legwork had already been done, and it was simply a matter of collecting evidence in Columbus and picking up the target for questioning. Of course, Fischer couldn't have known how much sanitizing Martinez had done to the file the night before, making sure to lay a careful trail of breadcrumbs without revealing any of the supernatural or illegal activities they had done to get answers.

"You've got a new case," Fischer broke the news and turned the file toward them. "Person of interest is Dr. Stephen Forester, PhD in biology, a US citizen who has spent the past twenty years in Ukraine. He returned four months ago, and is linked to three animals attacks that have resulted in two injured and one dead. The most recent attack was at the San Diego Zoo."

Lee opened the folder, moving it so that Rogers could see as well. There were photos, field notes, witness statements, filed requests for information—the whole shebang.

Fischer continued, "Forester just arrived in town yesterday, and the previous agents working the case believe the Columbus Zoo is his next target." His voice grated in his low register. "Besides having bad blood with OSU, Forester may also be targeting a retired professor that still lives in the city. I don't need to tell you how important the zoo is to the city, so I need you two to start immediately. Read up and get to work."

Rogers and Lee correctly interpreted that as a dismissal and left, file in hand. *So much for my plans tonight*, Rogers lamented before opening the folder.

*****

Ohio weather was a capricious thing; you could have all four seasons in one day, and it would shock no one native to the Buckeye state. While Columbus was generally spared the giant piles of lake effect snow—a fact that gave Clevelanders something to crow about along with the Browns and the Cavaliers—the bitter cold of the polar vortex had once again descended on central Ohio this winter. There was no doubt about it; Ohioans were ready for spring.

Camille Chevapravatdumrong looked out the bay window of her breakfast nook, spying the influx of birds gathering at the feeders. The high trills of the warblers floated above the syncopated chirps of the sparrows. If that wasn't enough of a harbinger of spring, her Magnolia tree was in bloom, painting her backyard with furled magenta balls that opened pale pink to white. In a few weeks, their fragrant scent would be gone and their leaves would become a trodden brown mess on the lawn, replaced by the odorous white blooms of dogwoods that littered the city.

Dr. C, as her students had called her for decades, was officially retired. She had always considered herself a curious person, and when the day had come that she simply no longer cared to ask more questions or dig deeper, she knew it was time. As big as Ohio State University was, it gossiped like a small village. As soon as Dr. C made overtures about "taking a step back" and "cutting back on commitments," the speculations had spread like wildfire. And as soon as she supported one of her PhD candidates forward as a lead on a study, instead of taking the reins herself, it was enough confirmation for the department.

She relinquished her office once she'd finished advising the last of her PhD students, and OSU bestowed on her the title of professor emerita. It was a touching gesture that conferred professional respect with no monetary benefit. She certainly wasn't expecting it, but as her youngest pointed out, it was the least they could do, considering all the grant money Dr. C had brought into the university over the years.

At first, Dr. C was determined to enjoy her retirement.

She was going to take vacations, pick up hobbies, take classes, see her grandchildren more—all the things she had deferred for work, but she'd unearthed many a truth since retirement. First, while she loved her grandkids dearly, she didn't necessary want to spend her golden years with crying babies and snotty toddlers—she had done her time. The older ones that were already in school weren't so bad, because they could basically take care of themselves and just needed an adult present for general supervision. No, Dr. C was solidly a "why don't you bring the kids over for a visit" rather than a "drop the kids off and I'll babysit" grandma.

Second, she wasn't a hobby person. Intellectually, she understood the purpose of having things you liked to do to pass the time that were supposed to bring you joy, but she had a hard time doing things that weren't necessary or important. While some people felt the need to create something or express themselves artistically, Dr. C had come to the conclusion that she was not one of them, after trying a slew of classes in every arts and craft discipline she could find.

Lastly, she had to be honest about her feelings regarding traveling—it was a pain! Granted, she liked seeing new things, but the enjoyment she derived often didn't balance out the annoyance of airports, taxis, luggage, hotels, notifying her credit card of travel dates, holding the mail, and making sure her cell phone would work at her destination.

When she was working, vacations were mostly to get away from the unrelenting lockstep of everyday life; they were the equivalent of running away from home, but within contained parameters. Now that she wasn't working and her kids were grown, she didn't really have much from which to escape. For the first time in decades, her day-to-day reality was completely of her own making—why would she need to get away from that? She could muster enthusiasm to travel twice a year if she spaced it out, but even then, she started longing for her own bed after a week. She wasn't sure when she became one of those people that had to sleep in their own bed, but she was of the age where she was wearing purple and anyone that didn't like it could kiss off.

That's where things had stood for Dr. C. Accomplished professor, scientist, researcher, and mother…and retired with more time on her hands than she knew what to do with. Fortunately, she had found out about a senior volunteering program and found a place at the Columbus Zoo. It gave her leisure time purpose, without being confining like a job. She got plenty of fresh air and physical activity, and she treasured her time spent with the animals.

Dr. C finished her tea and retreated to her bedroom, where she readied for work. Recently, she spent most of her time with the animals from the Heart of Africa exhibit while they were in winter retreat, waiting for the temperatures to finally warm enough to reintroduce them in their outdoor habitats. She changed out of her pajamas into her zoo gear, donning a padded vest for extra warmth. She brushed her short white hair, fondly remembering when it was thick, long, and jet-black.

Her house shoes shuffled on the wood floors as she traded them for her walking shoes.

Dr. C was doing her final possession check when her doorbell rang. She wasn't expecting anyone or anything; maybe one of her girls used her address? Sometimes they did that, knowing that she was likely to be at home for daytime deliveries. Dr. C peeked through the eyehole and saw two men dressed in suits. She opened the door without releasing the chain. "Hello?"

"Good morning. We are looking for Camille Chevapravatdumrong," Agent Lee rattled off without missing a syllable. Rogers had learned long ago that they got a better reaction if Agent Lee made first contact with Asians—it might be a little racist, but it worked.

"You are speaking to her," she replied officiously. "How can I help you?"

"I am Agent Jeremy Lee of the FBI and this is my partner, Kyle Rogers." They presented their badges and IDs. Dr. C turned a shrewd eye to them and nodded when she was satisfied. "We would like to speak with you, if now is a good time."

"I'm actually on my way out," she rebuffed them gently. *What does the FBI want with me?*

Agent Lee spotted the Columbus Zoo logo embroidered on her blue shirt. "You wouldn't be headed to the zoo, by any chance?"

"Yes," she responded, startled. "What is all this about?" she demanded.

"We have reason to believe you may be the target of a

person of interest we are tracking. I would strongly advise speaking with us before you go to the zoo, for your own safety," Lee chose his words carefully. It was a fine line between getting someone to take you seriously and freaking them out.

"Target?! Who on earth would be targeting me?" she asked, flabbergasted.

Finally, Rogers spoke, "Does the name Stephen Forester mean anything to you?" He deliberately left out her name to avoid butchering it.

Dr. C didn't answer and instead closed the door. The agents waited patiently, hearing the rattle of the chain on the other side. She opened the door wide this time. "You'd better come in."

Chapter Fifteen

Detroit, Michigan, USA
5th of April, 6:00 p.m. (GMT-4)

Martinez breathed a sigh of relief as she pulled into her driveway. The flight had been packed with intermittent turbulence, and traffic was a bear, but she was finally home. She pulled her luggage from the back, locked up her car, and let herself in, calling hello to her ethereal housemates. Sometimes she felt weird talking to ghosts, but it somehow felt rude not it—she knew they were there, even if they hadn't officially met.

All the food she had bought earlier this week had either gone bad or needed cooking—neither of which she had the energy to deal with tonight. She pulled her suitcase up the stairs and left it at the foot of her bed to sort later. Right now, all she was interested in was taking a long hot soak in the tub. After securing her gun from the hidden compartment in her luggage and reassembling it, Martinez turned on the taps and sprinkled in lavender salts before undressing.

She switched on some music, dimmed the lights, and tested the water with her fingertips before stepping into the claw foot tub. After a few minutes, she regretted not bringing a glass of wine, but she supposed she had to have *something* to draw her out of the tub.

Something had been bothering her about this case, but she had been too preoccupied to really give it thought until she was on her way back to Detroit. She was thrown off-balance in San Diego—one foot in the FBI, the other in the Salt Mine. It was nice to return to solid footing that she intimately understood—she could run a mundane investigation in her sleep—but other than blow a little salt, she really didn't do any magic or use the knowledge Chloe and Dot had been pumping into her for months. She was little more than a federal beard for Wilson's supernatural operation, which was fine—that was the mission they were assigned.

But it raised questions. What's it going to be like when she's on her own and she has to make the call: use mundane tools or pull out the esoteric guns? It made her wonder what she would have done in Wilson's place. He had no qualms breaking the law to obtain his objective, something Martinez wouldn't have considered when she was just an FBI agent. But although she had seen just a little of what was really out there, she was well aware that demons and other such creatures didn't have much regard for law and order. They wore people like skin suits and strung them up as marionettes. They invaded the core of your being and gleefully laughed the whole time.

She plunged her head under the water, hoping to drown out the doubts. When she emerged, she made herself a deal.

Tonight, she could mope, drink a little too much wine, and have ice cream for dinner. Tomorrow, she had to get to work.

Saturday morning came bright and early. Martinez started with a run and a hot breakfast; the stale bread on her counter was good enough for toad in the hole, and the orange juice in the fridge was still on this side of questionable. Her luggage was emptied, laundry started, and all the boxes unpacked and collapsed. She was here now; no more living in between. Covered in dust and sweat, Martinez took a quick shower and dressed for a casual day out: jeans, a light sweater with a jacket, and short boots.

She had only performed magic within the Salt Mine with Chloe and Dot, but the setup made it impossible to perform certain types of spells. For example, she couldn't practice charm spells because it was impossible to charm the twins—they were two minds sharing a body. The magical wards on the Mine prohibited movement from one plane to another, so conjuration, scrying, and teleportation were out of the question. That was why the twins used transmutation spells to find an agent's power—to change a superficial aspect of a thing that was already in front of you didn't violate the wards. The librarians had supplied Martinez with legitimate magical words and located her source of power. Now it was up her to put them together.

Her first stop was a bustling coffee shop, and she took a seat in the corner with her cappuccino. She decided to start small: inanimate objects. At first, the background noise and constant movement in her peripheral vision was distracting, but she used the mantra Chloe and Dot had discovered within her—*Hail Mary, full of grace, the Lord is with thee*. The first thing Martinez conjured was a spoon to stir some sugar into her coffee. She felt a tingle pass through her when it appeared at the side of her cup, like she could feel the world blink. She immediately turned her head, expecting others to have felt it or witnessed her perform magic, but they were blissfully unaware. Buoyed by her success, she bought an oversized cookie and practiced moving it, breaking it, and mending it with magic, taking bites intermittently to allay suspicion.

Fueled by a little caffeine and sugar, Martinez decided to step up her game and drove to the dog park. It was a sunny afternoon, if a little chilly when the wind picked up. She passed through the duel gate system and took a seat on a bench there two trails met. She hadn't tried using magic on any living thing more complex than a plant, and thought animals would be the next logical step. An overfriendly Labrador lumbered over to her and started slobbering on her jeans as he sniffed. Martinez drew from her well and inserted enchantment into her words. "Easy, buddy. I'm not going anywhere." The dog immediately backed down and lay on the ground. *Okay, that was too much. Dial it down.* Martinez held out her hand and tried to imagine the magic as a thread unwinding from a spool within her. "It's okay, you can sniff me. You just can't climb on top and drool on me." His ears perked up and he rose, gingerly approaching. His tail was waggling fiercely but the rest of him remained calm.

"Baxter, don't bother that nice lady!" A winded blonde ran down the trail. She stopped abruptly at the bench, in awe at how well behaved her dog was being. "He's never this calm around strangers," she marveled.

Martinez gave him a scratch behind the ears. "He's a friendly dog, if a little excitable."

Baxter's owner took a seat next to Martinez and spied the open field of dogs. "Which one is yours?"

"Oh, I don't have a dog." Martinez dropped the magic from her voice and Baxter returned to his rambunctious self, prompting the blonde to rein him in. "I travel a lot for work, and it wouldn't be fair to the dog. But I love 'em, so I come to the park to bask in other people's dogs."

Baxter's owner wasn't sure if it was sweet or a little creepy to show up at a dog park without a dog, but settled for sympathetic. "That's a shame. This is a really good park if you ever decide to get a dog of your own," she added, as she rose and called the Labrador to her side. Her relief at his obedience was palpable. "Have a nice day!" she called back to the bench.

Martinez stayed for another thirty minutes, practicing how to apply more or less magic smoothly. She made her exit after she stopped a German Shepherd from bullying a Boston Terrier on its way to the small dog pen. Her stomach growled, reminding her that breakfast had been hours ago and the cookie wasn't cutting it, regardless of its girth.

She wasn't sure if the slight headache was from hunger or mental fatigue from concentrating on her spells, but she was certain a little food and caffeine couldn't hurt. One chicken and avocado wrap washed down with mango ice tea later, Martinez found herself people watching from her perch at the counter. She toyed with the idea of trying her enchantments on people—it might be considered a public service if she silenced the jerk talking very loudly on his bluetooth earpiece or the kid that insisted on playing his music so loud that you could hear every beat drop through his earbuds. However, the general fatigue remained, even if her headache had subsided, and Martinez thought maybe she had done enough magic for the time being.

She stopped by the grocery store for a healthy load of perishables as well as a nice crusty loaf of bread for dinner. Martinez was a big believer of eating in season, and the first of the asparagus and peas were hitting the shelves. Soon, it would be salad days. She opened the cranberry walnut maple granola she'd bought from the bulk section and nibbled on a handful as she drove home, running down her to-do list before Monday came again.

She entered her quiet house and deposited the bags on the kitchen counter before kicking off her shoes. With the push of a few buttons, music filled the living room, one of the many stations that came with her TV package. She sifted through the pile of mail that had collected while she was gone—most were adverts and things addressed to "current resident" that went directly into the recycle bin. The washed clothes were moved into the dryer, and Martinez poured herself the last of the wine from the night before—it was time to cook.

Cooking was one of the things she had longed for during her stint living at a hotel. Her kitchen box, complete with herbs and spices, had been one of the first things unpacked, second only to her bed. When she was younger, she loved being in the kitchen and was given age appropriate tasks, like snapping green beans or peeling vegetables. In her adolescence, she had pushed against making food in a misguided search for finding importance in other areas that weren't "women's work." It was only after college that she had rekindled her interest in cooking, as she came to understand that what you put in your body is pretty damn important, regardless of who is making the meals.

Beyond healthy eating, it also gave her respite, time where her unconscious mind could work through things while her hands chopped, sliced, diced, stirred, and seasoned. In Portland, she had been able to cook dinner most nights, but clearly, her new job had more travel demands, often with little notice. She was going to have to cook big when she could, and freeze individual servings if she wanted to eat home-cooked meals and avoid wasting food.

The counter disappeared under a cascade of food pulled

from the grocery bags and cupboards. Martinez settled on making a big pan of lasagna and a pot of chili, both of which would freeze well once they cooled. Tears were shed when the onions were diced, flat white seeds made a mad dash in all directions as she opened and chopped the green bell peppers, and a sticky translucent film clung stubbornly to the garlic—which Martinez took as a sign of its freshness. Cans of tomatoes and tomato paste were stacked to one side, as well as jars of spices: rosemary, oregano, basil, marjoram, fennel, chili powder, Mexican oregano, salt, and pepper. The large tub of ricotta and bags of shredded mozzarella sat beside a pile of freshly grated parmigiano-reggiano. A large pot of salted water was slowly coming to a boil for the flat sheets of noodle while the pressure cooker containing red kidney beans rumbled. All in all, it was a glorious mess.

Once she had the pan of lasagna baking in the oven and the chili simmering on the stove, she lounged on the couch with a drink, flush from the warm kitchen. She had time to kill—lasagna always took longer than you thought, usually in increments of "fifteen more minutes!" All she had to do was toss the salad and slice the bread, and dinner was ready.

Martinez took the stack of collapsed boxes downstairs to the storage room next to the fuse box, and paused in front of the wooden planks covering the walls. To the uninitiated, that was all there was down here, but Martinez knew better. Wilson used to live here and he had required space for esoteric activities—what better place than a finished basement behind a heavily warded hidden door? Martinez blindly felt for the release latch and the far wall swung back.

She had rarely used the basement, only entering a handful of times to deposit the excerpts of books and scrolls Chloe and Dot had supplied her—those works that contained true words of power for those who knew how to perform magic. She pulled back a heavy light-blocking curtain that covered the doorway, and flipped the switch on the wall. The room flooded with soft bright light. It was one large room with a large flat sheet of thick slate mortared into the floor on the far side. There was plenty of recessed shelving built into the finished walls, but the place was otherwise bare—Martinez hadn't moved any of her furniture in here. The air lacked the musty, stale quality that permeated so many basements, thanks to the vents and air intake that kept things filtered and moving.

Martinez knew what this room was for: summoning. The smooth, level stone provided an ideal platform for chalking out protective circles with their intricate detail that demanded precision. Of all the ways to use magic, summoning seemed the most clear-cut: find the correct instructions and words of power for the being you want to summon, choose the correct circle, and be diligent in creating the protective sphere. Despite this, Martinez had been reticent to dabble in summoning. The only experience Martinez had with it beyond academic study was meeting Furfur, Great Earl of Hell, and in England at the country home of a demon-possessed medical examiner. One summoning had obviously worked properly while the other didn't, but both experiences were thoroughly unpleasant to say the least.

Maybe it was her Catholic upbringing, but making deals with devils and calling forth imps hardly seemed advisable. Still, summoning as a discipline had its merits and could be useful. It wasn't exclusively the domain of devils and demons; a practitioner could summon all manner of things: fey, ghosts, and maybe even figures of myth if you had the right instructions—Martinez had barely scratched the surface of uncovering what was real from the stuff of legends. She knew she would have to start somewhere; maybe she could start with something friendly.

Martinez grabbed a book and a piece of white chalk from the shelf. Wilson had left various tools when he moved, objects he wouldn't need at his new place where these things were etched into the floor itself—chalk, templates, overgrown versions of geometry tools to make drawing with precision faster and easier, and rags to wipe the slate clean between uses. She started on the circle itself—everything focused around the circle. She worked on the geometric patterns and carefully copied the sigils from her book. She triple checked everything before sitting cross-legged on the floor a few feet from the circle; she was definitely going to bring down kneepads and a chair.

She focused her will and started the incantation, repeating the words over and over until three ethereal figures appeared in front of her—a man, a woman, and a child. They were all dressed in plain old-fashioned clothing that was at least a hundred years out of date, if not older. Martinez stood to greet them.

"I apologize for calling you away from the attic, but I wanted to properly introduce myself. I am Teresa, your new housemate. Wilson has told me all about you. I'm so pleased to meet you."

Chapter Sixteen

Oklahoma City, Oklahoma, USA
7th of April, 6:00 p.m. (GMT-5)

Alexander Petrovich Lukin slid the steak knife through his tender-cut, seared-to-rare perfection. The asparagus tips were charred from the grill, seasoned with course sea salt, fresh ground black pepper, and a splash of lemon juice. The baked potato's white fluffy innards were smothered with butter, chives, and a dollop of sour cream that ran down its crispy salted exterior. The warm Parker House rolls sat blanketed in linen in a basket with more butter on the side. Lukin couldn't argue with the late-night comedian that called Oklahoma the armpit of America, but he could not fault its steak.

He had kept a low profile since burning Peter Melkin and picking up his new alias out of LAX. He kept track of Forester's rental car as it trekked east and spent its third night in Columbus, Ohio. Normally, Lukin would have already taken a flight there, but according to the tracking number, his package should have arrived in Siberia three days ago. With any luck, his next flight would cross the Atlantic, and he hoped his last American meal would be steak.

Lukin felt strangely at home among all this cowboy

culture—modern amenities, but everyone drove big shiny trucks and SUVs while wearing Stetson hats and cowboy boots. It felt serenely surreal to watch the suburban cowboy roam his concrete prairie. Once he'd found a good steakhouse, he kept coming back, taking the same table in the secluded back corner where he could see all the entrances and exits. He sipped his bourbon, and wished smoking inside restaurants wasn't prohibited in the States. He could have gone for a nice cigar after such a meal.

He drove his silver Ford F-150 back to his hotel, watching traffic in his mirrors for tails. He was the first to admit his procedure had become lax, but the presence of the FBI in San Diego snapped him back into prime form. Once he cleared his hotel room and checked for signs of entry and interference, he loaded up his Tor server and pulled out his key fob—the Ivory Tower didn't trust the anonymity of the dark web and nestled its own deep web within it.

The security code on the fob changed every ninety seconds, and entering the string of characters before they switched was challenging, especially on a touchscreen with autocorrect. He hovered on the authentication page when the fob characters flipped anew, and his thumbs furiously tapped and hit submit. It only took a few seconds for the dashboard to load. He had a new message: *Package invalid. Resend.* "*Pizdets,*" he cursed as he closed Tor and surfed the benign internet for flights to Columbus, Ohio.

Chapter Seventeen

Detroit, Michigan, USA
8th of April, 8:30 a.m. (GMT-4)

If there was one complaint Martinez had about her new job, it was the elevator. She understood the need for security, but having to present her eye and palm for scanning just to get the Salt Mine elevator moving was a serious pain in the butt, as was having to go up to the fourth floor just to have someone with the right authorization scan their palm and eye to grant you access to the sixth floor. Heaven help you if you forgot something in your office. All the other agents seemed to take it in stride, but it still stuck in her craw.

Martinez slung her bag with her notes over her right shoulder and carefully stacked the brown bags of confections inside—no one liked smooshed muffins. She didn't bake often, and when she did, it was imperative that she got the goodies out of the house as soon as possible before she ate them all—it was impossible to bake in reasonable amounts when you lived by yourself. Coffee in one hand, she rode the elevator up one floor, where LaSalle greeted her. She presented him with a bag of treats. "Homemade pumpkin chocolate chip muffins, baked last night."

The tall black man opened the bag and inhaled the spiced

aroma. "Thanks, I love muffins," he replied before he scanned his eye and palm and pressed the button for the sixth floor.

"They're made with whole wheat flour, so I guess I'm counting them as healthy?" Martinez added for the benefit of Leader, who struck her as a little granola.

LaSalle smirked, picking up her gist. "I'll let Leader know," he assured her as the elevator doors closed.

The sixth floor was the same as she had left it before going to San Diego. She veered down the hallway to Weber's lab and knocked on the open door. "Harold, it's Lancer. I brought muffins," she called out.

The inventor looked up from his work and flipped the magnification lenses off his glasses. "Good morning, Lancer. Muffins, eh? What's the occasion?" He slid off his stool and took the proffered sack.

"I had a good weekend and did some baking," she replied. "Hey, I used the vape pen last week—it worked like a charm." She appreciated that Weber chuckled at her Monday morning pun before taking his first bite.

"Excellent! About the pen and the muffins—very moist," he elaborated. "Any feedback?"

Martinez thought about it. "I was only able to make three passes before I was worried about running out of salt. Usually that's enough, but it would be nice to get more passes out of it before needing to refill the chamber."

Weber popped the rest of the baked treat into his mouth. He grabbed a pencil from behind his ear and took notes on a scrap a paper. "I'll see what I can do. Did you use the amulet or the rosary?"

"Not yet. Thankfully, no magical attacks or casting on the fly during this mission," she replied.

Weber shrugged. "They can't be all whiz-bang."

"I have to run—I'm meeting the twins. I'll let you know how it goes when I do use them," she promised.

"Please do," he mumbled halfway through his second muffin.

Martinez doubled back and cut through the stacks until she reached the librarians' desk. "You're late," Dot noted the time.

"Sorry about that—I was delivering baked goods. I brought you muffins, if it helps.

"You bake?!" Chloe exclaimed.

"What kind?" Dot inquired skeptically.

"Pumpkin chocolate chip," Martinez answered, holding out a bag to each twin—even though they were conjoined, they were very much their own person.

"That is so thoughtful!" Chloe said graciously.

"Chocolate's a good start," Dot commented, accepting Martinez's peace offering. "You look like you have news."

"After we finished up the case, I was able to do some magic this weekend," Martinez announced as she put down her coffee and bag and pulled up a seat.

"That's wonderful," Chloe praised her. "Tell us all about it."

Martinez walked them through the spells she'd used as they

partook. Chloe's cheerful disposition was unwavering as usual, and even Dot's attitude seemed to improve with a little sugar and chocolate.

"So, how did you feel afterward?" Chloe inquired when Martinez finished her account.

"I felt great! It was nice doing it, instead of just reading about it," she answered.

Chloe and Dot exchanged a quick glance. "What do you mean when you say 'great'?" Chloe asked coyly. "Do you mean relieved that it worked—"

"—or were you high as a kite?" Dot finished her sister's sentence. Martinez's brow furrowed. "You know: stoned off your gourd, rolling, tweaking, chasing the dragon, getting fried," she elaborated.

Martinez laughed out loud, in part at Chloe's expression with each euphemistic turn of phrase her sister spouted. "I know what you mean, Dot. No worries—it was solidly in the realm of personal satisfaction at a job well done."

The librarians breathed a sigh of relief and resumed eating. "Not that there's anything wrong with that," Chloe clarified, "But if you were so affected, we would need to work more extensively with you to tailor your magical practice."

"I mean, you *did* waltz in here with fresh-baked muffins," Dot came to her sister's defense, albeit obliquely.

"No offense taken," Martinez brushed it off. "So what are we working on today?"

Dot swiveled and pulled out a stack of books. "More

reading for you to round out your general knowledge on non-Greco-Roman magic."

"And since you've been practicing, I think it's time we talked about charming," Chloe added. "More specifically, how to approach enchantments on other people." Martinez pulled out her pen and notepad and started by putting the date at the top of the page.

"The brain is a tricky thing," Chloe began. "It fills things in all the time, so much so that magicians can take advantage of that feature. Technically, you can charm without speaking, by directing your magic at a person and using other cues, things like body language or eye contact."

"But that is a lot harder," Dot picked up. "If you can use language, you can make shifts much easier and can essentially trick their brain into thinking that what you are suggesting is in fact the truth."

"The more you know about your target, the better. That can include superficial things, like what they look like, their age and profession, family life, etc, but if you can understand some aspect of their personality, no matter how trivial, that's the jackpot," Chloe continued.

"The whole walk a mile in someone's shoes thing," Dot interjected.

"I think the word Dot is looking for is 'empathy,'" Chloe managed to say without being snide about it. "If the target thinks you 'get them' on some level, they are more likely to roll with the magic instead of fight it."

"That makes sense; like how the FBI uses psychology and profiling in investigations," Martinez drew a parallel to something she wholly understood. "What do you mean by fighting the magic?"

"The brain does *not* like to be messed with," Dot spoke, dusting off the crumbs from her shirt. "It can fight back and resist if it has reason to believe it's being tampered with—this is the foundation of magical defensive training, which we'll start shortly."

"That's why it's best to take a soft-power approach when you can," Chloe suggested. "If you apply sheer brute force, there is a higher likelihood that the target's brain will revolt against the magic."

"That said, if you need to bump them with a little more magic to get things started and then smooth it out, the brain will make the appropriate excuses to keep everything reasonable," Dot cut in.

Martinez scrolled down her list of questions from the past weekend. "How long can someone be affected? When I was at the dog park, as soon as I dropped the magic, the dogs returned to their normal selves."

"It depends on how you shaped the magic," Dot fielded this question. "As a general rule, the longer you power it, the higher the karmic kick, and once you are no longer actively powering the magic, all bets are off. The effects may linger after you are no longer feeding the spell, but if someone or something breaks the reality you created with your magic, the person is likely to come to their senses."

"There are some workarounds, but they are generally considered the most heinous of charm enchantments, basically akin to driving someone crazy." Chloe didn't bother to hide the disgust in her voice. "We call them 'earworms' for lack of a better term. You can essentially take some aspect of the person's interest or personality, and turn up the volume to eleven." Martinez smiled at Chloe's use of a *This is Spinal Tap* reference—no doubt Dot made her watch it.

"It basically turns a person into a manic obsessive—they don't eat, they don't sleep, they only think about and do whatever was triggered in their brain by the magic," Dot spoke with a hint of sympathy.

"Sounds very much like the Midas coin," Martinez noted. "It picked up whatever someone wanted and amplified it until the desire for it consumed them."

"All that glitters is not gold," Dot cited, and Chloe nodded in agreement.

Chapter Eighteen

Columbus, Ohio, USA
8th of April, 10:00 a.m. (GMT-4)

Camille Chevapravatdumrong refused to be afraid. That wasn't to say she was going to overcompensate into foolhardiness, but she wasn't going to let an old specter from the past or the FBI cow her into hiding. She had allowed the agents to make their case and express their concern, but she adamantly refused to stop going to the zoo or stay barricaded in her own home—she had her grandson's birthday party to attend this weekend! But she had made some concessions. She allowed them to post plainclothes officers in an unmarked car outside her house, and when she did work at the zoo, Agent Rogers—Kyle, when he was in his zoo khakis—would accompany her. She could use a little extra muscle in the giraffe barn without having to intrude on the other staff.

Dr. C had had many students over the years. Over time, their names and faces had become a blur, requiring a nudge to pull a specific individual from the mass her brain catalogued under the general classification of students. But there were some that stayed with you—you never forgot your first. She still remembered the day Stephen Forester came into her office; his long shaggy hair was slicked back and he was wearing his nicest slacks and a buttoned-down shirt. She had recently attained tenure and was only fifteen years older than him; she was touched at his attempt to put his best foot forward.

Part of her responsibility as a tenured professor—in addition to conducting research, securing its funding, publishing its findings, and teaching classes—was to develop the next generation of scientists and PhDs. She had agreed to let him work on the research team of her most recently funded study, and found him bright and dogged. After a trial period, she agreed to advise Stephen through his PhD. She came to lean on him more and more—he was competent, energetic, and generally pleasant to work alongside. It broke her heart to discover the missing blood samples. She would have never thought to do an inventory of the lab's freezers herself without a nudge from the department; Stephen had always taken care of things like that for her.

After some thought, Dr. C had decided not to tell any of her children about the return of her old pupil—it would have only frightened them. Ever since she entered her sixties, they had started treating her differently. She couldn't make a comment about forgetting something without them jumping to Alzheimer's or arrange a simple repair for the house without one of them showing up to make sure the workmen didn't take advantage of her. They frequently asked bizarre questions, like "are you taking your medicine," and "did you remember to eat?" The thought had crossed her mind that maybe she wouldn't need this blood pressure medication if she didn't have infuriating children, but she held her tongue. She knew she should be grateful for having family that cared—not everyone had that in their lives—but it was also a nuisance.

So, instead of cowering behind closed curtains, she had spent Saturday in the company of her kids and grandkids at an indoor trampoline center. Dr. C had plastered a pleasant noncommittal smile on her face while the gaggle of kids leapt, flipped, and screamed with glee. She had taken a few bits of Star Wars birthday cake and watched her grandson—now eight years old—gush over his newest lightsaber. When her daughter had given her a disapproving look, Dr. C had posited a philosophical inquiry—can a budding Jedi ever have too many?

On Sunday, she had gone to church, like she did every week. The sermon had been adequately thought-provoking in the weeks leading up to Palm Sunday and Easter, and the hymns familiar and soothing—she never had a good-enough voice to sing in the choir, and it was her chance to experience the sense of unity that came with singing in a group.

Which brought her to this morning. Dr. C took one last look at herself in the hallway mirror, keys in hand. She straightened her shoulders and uniform and made her way to the zoo.

*****

"Kyle, could you move the hay to the far pen for me?" It was technically a question, but Dr. C's phrasing intimated it was more an order than request. Agent Rogers buried the pitchfork into the mound before pushing the wheelbarrow down the hallway. He didn't mind the physical labor or the smell of manure—he had grown up in rural Ohio, spent years in 4H, and won more than his fair share of county fair ribbons. No, what really chaffed was that Lee wasn't doing it; Rogers would have paid good money to see his partner shoveling giraffe dung.

Rogers and Lee had reviewed the case files, and most of the evidence they were given was circumstantial at best. They could place Forester in the area around the time of the other attacks with a plausible if stretched motive, but there was no direct evidence that he had perpetrated them. The working theory was that he was cooking up his own salt licks and putting something in or on them that influenced the animals, causing them to attack. The previous investigators had gotten a little further in San Diego with eyewitnesses and footage confirming Forester delivered the salt to the enclosure, but without the actual salt lick, there was no proof that the salt had been tampered with.

After going around a few times, Rogers and Lee had

come to the conclusion that if they wanted to bring him in and charge him, they needed something definitive. When Dr. Chevapravatdumrong refused to not show up for work, the agents had to divide and conquer—one with each doctor. They had settled this the way they made all decisions that were up to them: Rochambeau. Rogers had thrown paper, Lee scissors, and the rest was history.

While Rogers became Dr. C's muscle behind the scenes, Lee kept eyes on Forester, tailing his Honda around the city and on foot around the zoo. Forester had spent every day at the zoo since they received the case, and Lee wasn't complaining about this stakeout—it beat living out of his car. Most people who spent the day at the zoo observed the animals, but Lee noted that Forester was more intent on watching the staff entrances and exits, deliveries, and shadowing the zoo staff as they made their rounds.

According to the file, Forester had delivered the salt lick to the enclosure at the San Diego Zoo, effectively letting the zoo administer it for him. If he stuck to the same MO, he would have to find a way to get the salt into the winter pens, and that's when they would pick him up in possession of the biological weapon—in this case, the doctored salt. It had been Roger's idea to call the lab at UCLA before they closed Friday afternoon to secure blood and tissue from the pronghorns for additional testing and examination before everything was destroyed—sure, it wasn't rabies, but if there was something else in there that matched whatever they found in the salt, it would strengthen their case. Lee had to admit, Rogers had his moments.

This morning, Lee was outside Forester's motel, waiting for him to make his daily excursion to the zoo. When Forester made one trip to his car and then returned to his room, Lee pulled up his binoculars for a better look. The first thing Lee noticed was Forester's attire; he had traded in his jeans and sweater for khaki pants and a blue shirt under a black vest, a spitting image of what the Columbus Zoo staff wore. Next, he noted the payload on Forester's right shoulder: a black duffle bag of significant weight, if Forester's hunched back was any indication. Forester gently deposited it in the back next to an identical bag before shutting the door. Lee called into the Columbus Field Office for plainclothes backup and sent a text to Rogers. *Target on the move with the package.*

*****

Stephen Forester had risen this morning feeling his age plus some. No amount of pills could roll back the years or the cancer spreading within him. He consoled himself with the thought that shortly, his work would be done. He was coming to the end of things; soon, everyone would see his work and rue the day they had stymied his progress. They would be sorry when he passed, and thought of all that could have been accomplished if only they had nurtured his genius.

Bolstered by this thought, he sat up and swung his legs over the edge of the bed. After he used the toilet, he checked the bottles—they had finally set! He pulled out the utility knife and carefully sliced off the top of the plastic bottles and down their sides. The desiccated salt soaked in the liquid and cured it into a solid piece that could be unmolded from the two-liter bottle. Rolling them into motel towels, he secured them two at a time into two duffel bags to lighten each load. He chose not to dwell on the fact that when he started this venture, he would have been able to carry all four in one bag.

He washed his hands before finishing the rest of his morning ablutions. His cheeks had sunken in, and it was becoming harder to recognize the old man that stared back at him in the mirror. He spied the zoo outfit he had set aside for when the big day came. A wave of nausea came over him in the excitement, but it was nothing a few dissolvable tablets under the tongue couldn't quell.

Forester retrieved the light blue shirt from the hanger, working the buttons with his stiff fingers. It was the same color as the zoo staff's shirts but missing the Columbus Zoo logo, a fact that he had intended to hide with his black vest—something he saw many employees wear to keep out the chill of the early morning. He tucked the ends into his khaki pants, securing them with a belt that was now still a little loose, even on the tightest setting. Forester inspected himself in the mirror—it only had to hold up for one visit, an hour in and out at most. And then he could rest.

He loaded the duffle bags one by one, saving his energy for when he had to carry them both into the zoo. He closed the door to his motel room and fired up the Honda's engine. He pulled onto the city loop and exited for Powell, but instead of following the signs for the zoo, he took the back roads, leading to the area where deliveries were made and employees parked.

He pulled off to the side of the road, just a hundred yards from the lot where they parked the golf carts. Much like the city of Columbus itself, the zoo had sprawled since he had last been there and was almost 600 acres; the golf carts made covering the distances more manageable. Forester popped the back door of the car and hoisted a bag on each shoulder, shuffling his way through the gate.

They were heavy, but Forester persisted, unloading the bags in the first cart he saw that had the keys in the ignition. There was an unmanned clipboard and walkie-talkie on the dash, but Forester didn't stick around to find out who was derelict in their duties. He turned the key and followed the concrete pavement that ran on the backside of the zoo where the visitors couldn't roam. He was headed for the Heart of Africa.

Forester had done as much research as he could online before he actually showed up at the zoo. With all African animals in their respective barns for the winter, it would be easier to target a specific species. With the savannah closed, the traffic in the area should be minimal both in terms of visitors and ancillary staff. Once he found out Dr. C worked with the giraffes, through one of her colleagues' social media posts and pictures—#blessed—it was simply a matter of planning. The giraffe barn was built within the Heart of Africa exhibit, but in the back, only available to the public if they shelled out more money for behind-the-scenes access. It would be a simple matter of entering, dressed as a zoo employee, and depositing the salt in their pens. Forester imagined the terror of a coordinated giraffe attack; if Dr. C was caught in the middle of it, all the better.

Forester cruised down a walkway that led to the barn in question. It loomed tall, which was unsurprising given its inhabitants, but it was also quite deep, with a private outdoor pen to the side. He slowed to a halt in front of a pair of doors marked "zoo staff only." His heart raced as the adrenaline pumped through him; he was so close. He stilled his shaking hands, picked up the first bag, and reached for the barn door. Once opened, sirens and lights started and armed figures came from everywhere on both sides of the door. A clear and steady voice rang out in the late morning air, "FBI. Drop the bag, Mr. Forester, and put your hands up."

Chapter Nineteen

Columbus, Ohio, USA
8th of April, 1:30 p.m. (GMT-4)

After waiting more than thirty minutes for a rental car, Lukin breathed a sigh of relief as the John Glenn Columbus International Airport was finally behind him. His first priority was to get eyes on Forester, and the tracker on his Honda pegged the car around the backside of the Columbus Zoo and Aquarium. Lukin took this as a good sign—if Forester was at the zoo, that meant he was planning another attack, which gave Lukin another shot at obtaining the objective. He entered the coordinates of Forester's car and followed the GPS on his phone rather than use the rental car's; it looked like he was going to be in the States a little longer, and it never hurt to be cautious.

Lukin had a bad feeling as soon as he saw the flashing lights and road barricades. Local traffic was being diverted through a detour, and Lukin followed the line of cars crawling through the squeeze. Everyone was rubbernecking, so his curiosity didn't seem out of the ordinary, but the string of Russian expletives he muttered under his breath was gloriously graphic.

In his rearview mirror was Forester's obsidian blue pearl Honda CR-V, crawling with FBI.

He turned on the radio and searched for a local news station. He got a weather report and traffic update, but nothing about the zoo. Lukin found his way back to the highway and headed to a hotel to regroup. He was about to turn off the DJ prattle when a newsbreak came over the air about a federal raid at the Columbus Zoo. Lukin turned the knob up instead of off. "Federal investigators apprehended a suspect at the Columbus Zoo earlier this morning. Special Agent James Fischer of the Columbus Field Office has released a statement that 'the nature of the threat is isolated and has been neutralized.' The zoo has closed for the rest of the day, but Columbus Zoo and Aquarium representatives want to reassure the public that visitor and animal safety is their top priority and they have every intention of opening tomorrow for normal business hours. Traffic around the zoo continues to be slow due to street closures and detours."

Lukin shook his head and swore, "*Zhizn' ebet meya*."

*****

Stephen Forester sat stone-faced, staring at his reflection in the one-way mirror. Rogers found the cold blank stare disturbing, and wondered what sort of mind was working behind those sunken eyes. Lee opened the door and joined Rogers with an update. "The lab received the blood and tissue samples from UCLA before lunch. The salt licks have been entered into evidence and are being taken to the lab for processing, as well as the empty bottles found in Forester's motel room." Lee looked through the glass at their still suspect. "Has he said anything?"

"Not a word, and it's freaking creepy," Rogers answered.

"Has he asked for a lawyer?"

"Nope. Just sits there, glaring." Rogers took a sip of his cup of late afternoon caffeine. "It doesn't make any sense," he muttered.

"Why is that?" Lee asked as a matter of routine while he flipped through the file in his hand.

"If you were hell-bent on revenge for a wrong that happened over twenty years ago—so much so that you flew back into the country for the first time since you left—why would you use animals? A straight-up assault, plus or minus a weapon—sure—but animals? They are unpredictable, with a will of their own."

"Crazy is as crazy does," Lee adapted the Gump-ism to match the determined scientist on the other side of the glass. As far as Lee was concerned, it was highly unlikely that Forester was a stupid man. "Let's go in and introduce ourselves; see if we can't get a few answers."

Rogers stood and threw his empty cup in the trash. Even though he had changed out of his zoo uniform and back in his suit, he couldn't do much to remove the smell of animals and hay that lingered on him. Lee entered first, taking confident strides to the opposite side of the table from Forester. Rogers followed and closed the door behind him.

Lee dropped a thick file on the table before unbuttoning his jacket and taking a seat. Lee was a good agent, and he had a unique way of breaking the recalcitrant with the weight of his disapproval, expressed not only in words, but tone, body language, and demeanor. The act even put Rogers on edge the first few times he had seen it. For Lee, it was easy; he merely impersonated his Korean father-in-law—it worked every time.

"I am Agent Jeremy Lee. This is my partner, Agent Kyle Rogers. This interview is being recorded. For the benefit of the recording, I am reminding you of your right to legal counsel and that you have previously waived this right. Could you please verify that you have been offered and declined a lawyer?" Forester didn't break his gaze at some fixed point behind them.

Lee continued, "Are you Stephen Elliot Forester, PhD of Biology and Department Head at the Institute of Molecular Biology and Genetics of the National Academy of Sciences of Ukraine?" Forester twitched at the sound of his credentials, but remained mute. Lee produced a copy of Forester's US passport and fingerprints that verified his identity.

"Dr. Forester, what brought you to the restricted area of the Columbus Zoo this morning?" Lee produced photos of Forester entering the delivery gate and stealing the golf cart, black duffle bags in plain sight. Again, there was no answer.

Rogers spoke up, "Mr. Forester, things will go better for you if you cooperate with us."

"It's Dr. Forester," the suspect broke his silence. "I didn't achieve the pinnacle of my field to be addressed as 'mister.'" Lee chuckled to himself—Rogers always had a knack for finding people's buttons.

"My mistake, Dr. Forester," Rogers apologized. "Why don't you tell us what's in the salt. Our lab is analyzing it as we speak, so it's only a matter of time before the jig is up."

Forester's impassive mien broke into uncontrollable laughter, light and lyric at first but it quickly turned bitter and mocking. "Your lab? You think some FBI lab flunkies can even begin to comprehend my work?!"

Lee leaned in and pried his way into the crack Rogers had made in the facade. "Why don't you enlighten us, Dr. Forester?"

One thought kept rolling through Forester's mind in the hours since his arrest at the zoo: *It's over.* At first, he was indignant—how dare they interrupt his magnum opus? Then, he was angry—he was so close to finishing what he'd started! Soon, his analytical mind kicked in and he clammed up. If he said nothing—gave them nothing—they would flounder in the dark. Alas, he was unaware of the case that had been built against him even before he arrived in Columbus.

Now it was dawning on the good doctor that there would be no getting out of this, no second chance for him. There would be no way to make the past right, but there was still time to explain. "If I answer your questions," Forester started with a calculated pause, "can I get a phone call?"

"You can have a phone call now if it is for legal counsel, Dr. Forester," Lee reminded him.

A short snide jeer escaped Forester. "No, I don't want a lawyer. They won't do me any good. I want to call my daughter, explain to her what happened in my own words."

Lee sat back and dropped his hands into his lap, relaxing his stance to draw Forester in. "I think that can be arranged, Dr. Forester, but first, we would also like to hear what happened. In your own words."

Forester thought for a moment. He was so tired. He was a dead man walking—did it really matter what he said or didn't say? He would spend more time in hospice than jail. "It's a rather long story and I'm a sick man. If you could recover the medication taken from me earlier, the one for nausea, it will make this easier."

Lee nodded his head, signaling to someone on the other side of the one-way mirror. "It will take a moment, but consider it done. Tell us about the salt, Dr. Forester."

*****

Lukin paced up and down his hotel room, cracking his knuckles. With Forester in custody, there wasn't going to be another animal attack. He considered returning to Russia and calling it an operational failure, but Lukin was fully aware of how unfavorably the Interior Council viewed nonsuccess. Which left him few options.

He had a notion and delved back into the dark web for information—he knew his idea was foolhardy, but he wanted to see if it was possible. After hunting down the necessary schematics, blueprints, and protocols, Lukin made an executive decision—if the Ivory Tower wanted something from Forester, they could get it out of him themselves. The steep cost and high risk did not appeal to him, but it was the mission objective that ended his time in America.

The Russian took a look at the map and made arrangements for later tonight, putting an offer price high enough to compensate for the short notice. Once he found his takers, he closed his Tor browser and fired up his banking app, scheduling a large transfer for tomorrow to a children's orphanage he patronized. He was going to burn through a lot of karma in the near future.

Chapter Twenty

Detroit, Michigan, USA
9th of April, 12:00 a.m. (GMT-4)

As Martinez slept soundly in her bed, the residents of the attic stirred as the witching hour turned. They didn't have beds, per se, but roused from a slumber of sorts. Wolfhard started where he left off yesterday morning in a disapproving tone, "As I was saying, don't you find it a little odd that she summoned us?"

Millie was straightening her ethereal skirt and apron. "Wolfhard, you make it sound like she summoned us to trap us into an item. It was simply a precaution; you can never be too careful whom you invite in." Wolfhard winced at the slight hint of recrimination in her words— almost two hundred years together, and she still wouldn't let him forget who invited their killer in. Millie retied the scarf around her neck, covering the spectral wound while she continued, "After all, Teresa didn't know us. If she had asked those two young men who lived here before her, they would have given her a less-than-favorable impression of us." Millie found it easier to be generous now that she no longer had to tolerate the previous raucous tenants.

Wolfhard lit his ephemeral pipe. "But Mr. Wilson spoke

to her about us," he pointed out. "I'm sure he vouched for us." The silent one played with her translucent dolly with the button eyes. She picked at the loose thread on the right, pretending not to listen.

"You know how honorable I find Mr. Wilson, but he doesn't burden himself with the formalities of etiquette. He could have brought her up to the attic and introduced us properly, but he didn't. Bless his heart, it probably didn't even occur to him," Mollie noted graciously before turning her attention to the silent member of their trio. "If you keep pulling, she's going to lose an eye," she warned.

"She does seem quite amiable," Wolfhard conceded with a puff of smoke. "Always says goodbye when she leaves in the morning and hello when she returns." The girl squirmed as Millie tried to tame her ghostly knots into a plait.

"She did apologize for waking us, and seemed amenable to the idea of coming up to the attic next time she wants to speak to us," Millie added.

Wolfhard knew which way the wind was blowing, but felt the need to go through the motions nonetheless. "So, what do we think?"

"She's quiet, nice, and thoughtful," Millie voiced her opinion. "And she likes to cook," she added without explanation, as if the statement spoke for itself. The silent one nodded seriously in solidarity.

"That settles it—we like her and she can stay," Wolfhard

announced, blowing a smoke ring with a mischievous grin. "Pity, it felt nice to move things again."

"She *does* give us her blessing to haunt anyone who breaks in," Millie consoled him. The silent one smiled as she finally plucked the thread out and the ghostly button dropped to the ground.

Chapter Twenty-One

Powell, Ohio, USA
9th of April, 1:00 a.m. (GMT-4)

It was a slow Monday night at the Powell Police Department, and Officer Mosley was knee deep in a thick textbook, drumming his pencil on the front desk between sips of lukewarm coffee. He hated the night shift and couldn't wait to take the sergeant's exam next month; it would be nice to no longer be the low man on the totem pole. The saving grace of his shift was that it was a slow night—the few weekend drunk and disorderly were already cleared by the time he reported for duty, giving him plenty of time to study on the clock. The only person they had in lockup wasn't even one of theirs—it was an FBI suspect waiting for transfer to the Cincinnati field office.

Mosley had heard about the raid on the zoo earlier; Powell was a small town, and news traveled fast. He was surprised they were holding the suspect on behalf of the Columbus FBI Office; apparently, as a resident agency, they didn't have cells for holding people and they used local law enforcement stations while they arranged transport to a federal facility. Their go-to was usually one of the Columbus PD precinct stations, but apparently, there was some dust-up between the FBI agents and the CPD's chief about liability, if the officer at shift change could be believed.

Typical, Mosley thought without a trace of irony. *Everyone in Columbus has to make a federal case out of everything.* Even though Powell was just north of the state capital, it was its own city and operated under its own jurisdiction. Even though he had his sights on greater things, he didn't feel the call of the city—the traffic, the cost of living, the constant influx of new people drawn to either to OSU or city life—no thanks.

The electronic ding of the front door interrupted his inner monologue before it could become a tirade. He looked up from the desk and saw a man dressed in a suit. He was rather unremarkable—brown hair, brown eyes, average height and build, clean-shaven—utterly forgettable. He approached the front desk and greeted Mosley in a pleasant baritone with a hint of Midwestern drawl in it. "Good evening, Officer. I'm here for the prisoner transfer."

Mosley felt discombobulated for a second, but it quickly passed. *I gotta lay off the coffee when I work nights*, he thought to himself, pushing the remains of his cup away. "Certainly, if you could just show me your ID and paperwork, we can get started."

The man's brow knitted in confusion. "But Officer, I just showed you my credentials, don't you remember?" Mosley blinked. Of course he had shown him. How could he forget?

"Sorry, I don't know where my head is tonight," he apologized.

"No problem," the man quickly forgave him. "Night shift is always a bear. You working alone?"

"For now. The others on patrol will float in and out, and the on-call sergeant's just a phone call away," Mosley answered more effusively than usual. He wasn't sure why he was so chatty all the sudden, this poor sod probably just wanted to get his man and get on his way. "If you'll just sign here for me, verifying you are you and here to pick up Dr. Forester—for our records," he explained, and handed him a clipboard with a cheap ballpoint pen attached.

"But Officer, I just signed them. See there?" the gentleman corrected him. Mosley looked at the paperwork again and, as plain as day, there sat a cursive scrawl on the dotted line.

Mosley shifted nervously—what the FBI must think of their small town operation! "Right, that all looks good." He straightened the paperwork officiously to regain some credibility. The officer rose from his chair, pulled open the door otherwise locked from the lobby, and let the gentleman through. Mosley reached for a set of keys. "Follow me."

The pair silently walked back to the holding cells, and the man in the suit made note of the cameras in the hall and in front of the locked and barred choke points, but said nothing. Mosley slung the keys around the ring until he found the right one. "Up and at 'em, Forester. Your ride is here," he called to the recumbent figure. Groggy and exhausted, Forester roused slowly.

"Dr. Forester, I'm here to take you to your next destination." The rich baritone vibrato filled the cells and reverberated against the walls, snapping the doctor to attention. Forester rose stiffly and placed his hands through the slot for cuffing; he had become inured to the routine, being moved from place to place all day yesterday. "I don't think that will be necessary, Dr. Forester. You aren't going to run, are you?"

"Nah," Mosley answered for the prisoner. "He's been quiet as a lamb since we got him." Forester nodded whole-heartedly in agreement and retracted his hands. Mosley turned the key, and the cell door came open. "If you'll come with me to processing, I'll get you his personal effects."

Officer Mosley ushered them to another part of the precinct and passed behind a door marked "Authorized Personnel Only." Forester waited next to his escort as Mosley rummaged through the shelves and found Forester's sealed manila folder. "Here we are," he said, as he began to open it for proper accounting.

"That won't be necessary. I'm sure it's all there," the man in the suit spoke with assurance. "We appreciate you holding him until we could arrange transport. As a friendly tip from one night shift worker to another, you should probably erase the security tapes from tonight. Wouldn't want the FBI poking their noses into your precinct's affairs. They can be a real pain in the ass—I should know!"

Mosley let out a deep belly laugh; he liked the cut of this guy's jib. "That's not a bad idea."

"You should go take care of that as soon as we leave," the man said knowingly, like they were confederates in a scheme.

"Will do," Mosley confirmed. "And you drive safe. There are a lot of wackos out there."

The gentleman, who held Forester by his upper arm, tipped his head toward Mosley and winked. "Don't I know it."

Chapter Twenty-Two

Detroit, Michigan, USA
10th of April, 6:06 a.m. (GMT-4)

Wilson stirred as the US Postal Service fleet collectively started their engines in their depot across the street from his private sanctum sanctorum at 500 10th Street. It was still dark out, but Wilson knew it was time to rise—he had used the rumbling vehicles as an alarm during the workweek since moving to his heavily customized converted warehouse, except for those holidays where mail wasn't delivered. Unsurprisingly, the Salt Mine worked those days—the supernaturally inclined rarely planned their plots around the federal calendar.

He rose and jumped straight into his morning stretches, limbering up for the day and getting his blood pumping before grabbing his coffee—already brewing in the kitchen—and breakfast. Within a half hour of waking, he was dressed for work—coffee cup in one hand, Korchmar Monroe attaché in the other—and descending the ornately adorned wrought iron spiral staircase that connected his fourth-story apartment to the ground floor of the warehouse. Besides a floating walkway along the third-story windows, there was no second or third floor, and the silver runes and sigils inlaid into the staircase and fireman's pole next to it ensured the penthouse remained off limits to supernatural forces other than those he wished— simply another precaution in his line of work.

The metallic British racing green 911 was waiting for him just where he'd parked it. Wilson deposited his attaché in the passenger's seat, settled himself in the driver's seat, locked all the doors, and started the engine. Only then did his raise the garage door—a massive six tons of steel, with teeth on its bottom that locked into the ground like a jaw. Wilson took security seriously, and it was the only entrance into and out of the 500. Once outside, he waited until the door completely closed before heading to the Salt Mine.

His day was starting out blissfully routine. He breezed through the gate guard with minimal chitchat. Abrams was in a chipper mood, although she still insisted on scanning his gun and case before buzzing him through. There were no green envelopes with red lettering in his in-basket waiting for him when he entered his office. He would have time to finish and submit his report before moving on to more interesting pursuits.

Wilson tucked away his attaché and fired up his computer. While it booted, he opened the well-worn manila folder and flipped through the dailies—an intel update culled from their larger CIA and FBI briefings. The olive box on the corner of his desk flashed and buzzed, drawing his attention. He pressed the button. "This is Wilson."

LaSalle's voice came over the speaker, "We have a communication from the lab regarding the tubes of blood you sent from San Diego; they asking for more information about the sample."

Wilson put the dailies aside. "Why?"

"Apparently, they found a unique molecule not yet encountered in nature," he answered. Wilson could tell he was quoting something from the pause preceding the awkward turn of phrase.

"Shall I reach out to them using my FBI credentials?" Wilson suggested.

"That would be fine," LaSalle replied before rattling off a phone number and name of contact.

There was an inverse relationship between interconnectivity and security, and as a general rule, the Salt Mine erred on the side of security. For example, the phones in the Salt Mine were good old-fashioned analogue landlines, and none of the computers had a connection to the exterior world—it was a closed intranet. There was no wifi or cell coverage once you went into the depths of the mine. It wasn't that the Mine eschewed technology, it was just selective about how it was implemented. As mobile technology flourished and agents needed to access or receive caches of information in the field, the eggheads had to come up with adaptive solutions that maintained the spirit of isolation and secrecy, not to mention the useful apps Weber helped design for spycraft. But the day-to-day work in the Mine? It was like stepping back in time, and Wilson was pretty sure productivity didn't suffer from the inability to check in with one's electronic crutch throughout the day.

Wilson picked up the ancient phone's receiver and punched in the number. After a brief hold, he was connected to the FBI lab that processed the blood sample he had sent to the Salt Mine.

"Hello, Dr. Bronwyn speaking," a feminine voice answered.

"Yes, this is Special Agent David Wilson. I got a message the lab had questions about biologic samples I sent for analysis last week."

"Oh!" she exclaimed. "I'm so glad you called. I have so many questions. First, where did you get it?"

"It was obtained during the course of an investigation. It's pronghorn blood from a recent animal attack at the San Diego Zoo."

"Ah yes, we also received blood and tissue samples from UCLA," she commented. "I didn't realize they were from the same animals."

"I'm no longer assigned to the case, so it's entirely possible the new agents working it duplicated some work," Wilson replied curtly. "Out of curiosity, what was so unique about your initial findings?"

"I don't know how good your biology is, but basically, we found a virus that isn't acting like a virus," she answered cryptically.

"Could you go into more specifics?" Wilson prodded her, picking up a pen and grabbing a notepad.

Dr. Bronwyn was both surprised and pleased at the request; most agents were not interesting in *her* shoptalk, just what it meant to their case. "Well, most viruses are just bits of DNA or RNA. Once they get inside a host cell, their simple structure allows them to get into the host cell's nucleus. Once the virus is inside, it hijacks cellular protein production, and the cell starts making more of the virus instead of the stuff it usually makes. Eventually the cell dies because it's not getting any of the things it needs, and when it bursts open, it floods the area with more of the virus. That's how viruses reproduce.

"In the blood you sent us, we found a molecule that looks like a virus in structure, but when it slips into a host cell's nucleus, the cell doesn't make more of the virus. It's interacting with the host's DNA, but I'm not sure how yet. My hypothesis is that it changes what proteins the cell makes from the cell's own DNA, but that's just a theory," she qualified.

Wilson's intuition kicked in. "What led you to that line of thinking?"

"I found extremely elevated levels of inflammatory markers and certain hormone levels correlating with high-stress states. The inflammatory pathway has a hair trigger, probably due to its role in the immune system. Once you start having the right combination of cortisol, cytokines, and interleukins floating around in the blood, the inflammation cascade activates and creates more inflammatory markers. It's basically calling for more reinforcements. That process can even change the neurochemical landscape," she reasoned.

Wilson jotted the information down as fast as he could using his own version of shorthand. "Neurochemical—you mean the brain?"

"Yes, all the neurotransmitters that affect mood, behavior, perception, and decision making. Now that I know it was from an animal attack that was vicious enough to warrant euthanasia and rabies testing, some of the results I found make more sense. With the additional blood and brain tissue, I can run more tests and see if there were any changes in the neurotransmitter levels."

Wilson tapped the end of his pen on the pad. "Could it be engineered? The person of interest is a molecular biologist by profession."

"It is most definitely engineered, otherwise the molecule would die out—it can't make more of itself to survive. The only reason we found it was the extensive testing that was ordered, including microscopy."

"Microscopy?" Wilson puzzled.

"Actually looking at it through a microscope," she answered. "Much of the modern testing often relies on knowing what you are looking for. When you don't have a clue and you just want to see what is there, nothing beats a high-powered microscope."

Wilson looked back over his notes. "Are you suggesting that someone engineered a virus-looking thing that stressed the animals to the point of attacking?"

"That is one possible explanation," Dr. Bronwyn replied neutrally, but the broad smile on her face demonstrated her relief that he'd put the pieces together on his own—if he didn't make her say it out loud, she could maintain a reasonable objective stance in the conversation. "But, there is a lot more testing to do before I have a shred of evidence to back that up." Wilson's silence on the other line prompted her to speak. "It sounds like a sci-fi movie plot, doesn't it?"

"I've heard of crazier things," he responded. "How many Sharknado movies are they up to now?"

Dr. Bronwyn chuckled. "Thanks for returning my call and helping put the samples into context. I suppose I'll be working with the agents assigned to the case from here on out."

"No problem, Doctor. Glad to be of help," Wilson said, before exchanging a few pleasantries and then hanging up.

No sooner had Wilson set down the receiver than a knock landed on his closed door. He rose to answer and was greeted by Martinez holding a stack of papers in her hands. She blurted out, "Have you read the dailies?" but stayed in the hallway until Wilson motioned for her to enter.

Wilson closed the door behind her. "I started, but had to make a phone call. Why?"

"Stephen Forester escaped FBI custody," Martinez replied,

taking a seat on the red leather chair opposite his desk. Wilson scrambled to his chair and flipped to the page she held open with her thumb. "He was being held at the Powell Police Department awaiting transport to the Cincinnati FBI Field Office and walked out of the station. The officer on night duty claims that a gentleman came to collect Forester for transport early yesterday morning with all the paperwork in order, only no one from the Cincinnati or Columbus Field Offices knew anything about it, and no paperwork or signatures regarding the transfer were found at the police station. The security video from that night has been wiped, and the officer gave the most vanilla physical description I've ever read. Call me suspicious, but that screams magic to me."

While Martinez paused to take a breath, Wilson skimmed the details—it had to be Lukin. That's how Wilson would have done it. "That's not our only hiccup. I just spoke to the lab about the pronghorn blood samples. Apparently, Forester has a little Doctor Moreau in him." Martinez leaned forward with intent curiosity as Wilson filled her in. She recognized some of the words Wilson read off his notepad from the academic articles and research she'd conducted while looking into Forester.

"Oh, this is bad," she sighed, putting the pieces together in her mind.

Wilson folded his arms with resignation, "Well, it doesn't look like the case was actually closed after all."

"Wait, you have the address of the lab Lukin was going

to send the pronghorn blood to. Couldn't we go there? Blow something up?" Martinez grasped at straws. She didn't come from the CIA, but she was pretty sure that was somewhere in their playbook.

"There's a chance Lukin took Forester there, but it could just be the lab they used to process the blood sample," Wilson pointed out. "It would be like someone blowing up the FBI lab we sent the pronghorn samples to—that doesn't target me or the Salt Mine. Plus, Siberia is littered with labs. It's east of the Urals with a low population density and cold weather for easy and cheap preservation—pretty much the perfect setup for the Russians to do whatever they want without interference or prying eyes. It's where they stash both their small pox and their Jurassic Park lab."

The room fell silent as they were both lost in their own thoughts. "Which one of us has to tell Leader?" Martinez asked reluctantly.

"I'm the one that pulled the plug too soon; I'll tell her. But all is not lost—I have the sample of Forester's hair that I took from his hotel room," Wilson spoke, calculating. "What's your schedule like today?"

"Training with Chloe and Dot in half an hour, then self-study," Martinez answered.

Wilson checked his Girard-Perregaux—he could go home, perform the summoning, and return with enough time to report his findings before end of day. "I'm going to run back to my place and see if I get anything off the hair. I should be back by two this afternoon. If I get a hit on Forester, we're good."

"And if you don't?" Martinez inquired.

"Then he's either dead or shielded by the Ivory Tower," he responded plainly.

Martinez rose and left Wilson's office to get ready for her appointment with the librarians, fondly remembering the days when wishing for death wasn't the better of two evils.

*****

David LaSalle came out to the lobby and found Wilson and Martinez waiting. "Leader will see you now." The agents followed LaSalle's hulking form to Leader's office, and her assistant-cum-bodyguard announced their entrance, "Fulcrum and Lancer here to see you."

"Thank you, David," she replied automatically. When the door shut, her hawkish eyes settled on them. "I understand you have an update."

Wilson kept his composure and spoke plainly, "Since turning the animal attack case over to the FBI, new developments have come to light. First, the lab has identified an engineered virus-like molecule that could possibly be responsible for the uncharacteristic aggression in the affected animals. It is not magical, but it is concerning that the Ivory Tower was interested in it. Second, Dr. Forester escaped FBI custody early yesterday morning in what appears to be a magically enhanced effort. However, I was able to scry Forester's location, so all is not lost. At the time of scrying, he was in a laboratory in Irkutsk, Siberia, the same one Lukin tried to send the pronghorn blood to."

Leader spun her chair around so that they could only see the back of her head bent down in thought. Martinez debated on whether that was a good or bad thing; when she looked over at Wilson, she couldn't tell from his face. After a minute, Leader lifted her head and tilted it to one side. "Is the physical evidence from the bust secure?"

"Yes," Martinez answered. "I made some discreet inquiries and they are currently at the Ohio FBI lab being processed."

"As are the only remaining blood and tissue samples from the pronghorns," Wilson added.

Leader turned back around, and much to Martinez's surprise, she was relieved to see Leader's impassive mien unmarred by anger or disappointment—such was Leader's effect on people. Leader buzzed her assistant. "David, the animal attack case has just become eyes only. Official cover is that Special Agents Wilson and Martinez of the FBI are retaking the lead. All physical and digital evidence should be forwarded to their care."

"Is there anything else?" LaSalle's tenor carried over the sound of his typing.

"Yes, please arrange ASAP travel to Helsinki for the Watson

and Marvel aliases, and then roundtrip tickets to Irkutsk, Siberia for the Charlotte and David Williams aliases: three nights at a hotel, honeymoon suite. Book them first class if you have to—time is of the essence. Arrange the appropriate documents and have the analysts gather what we know about the laboratories at the National Institute of Molecular Biology in Irkutsk. Reach out to our contact for entry."

The click of LaSalle's furious typing eventually came to a stop when he finally announced, "Consider it done."

Leader finally addressed her agents. "Pack for cold. You're headed to Siberia. No loose ends."

Chapter Twenty-Three

Listvyanka, Siberia, Russia
13th of April, 2:00 p.m. (GMT+8)

Martinez burrowed deeper into her insulated winter jacket and snuggled closer against Wilson. Per instructions, they choose outdoor seating in a covered alcove that blocked out most of the wind. The blanket across her lap and the radiant space heater helped, as did the sunny day, but it was still April in Siberia. They sat side by side, their backs to the restaurant's bank of windows, and they had an unfettered view of Lake Baikal in the distance.

"I'm not sure how much more of this beautiful pristine landscape I can take," she kept her voice low, as there was another couple dining outdoors.

His rubbed her far arm with his gloved hand and tilted his mouth toward her ear. "We can retreat to the hotel once we meet our contact."

Martinez smiled, daydreaming of her flannel pajamas and the large fireplace in their honeymoon suite, registered under David and Charlotte Williams—the now-married aliases they had used while investigating a caterer in England, back when they were merely engaged. Martinez wasn't sad to be reunited with the two-carat princess-cut diamond solitaire set in a white gold, complete with matching wedding ring—regardless of her feelings about matrimony, she didn't mind the bling.

"Who would have thought to marry our fictional identities?" she whispered into his neck.

"Coming in as tourists is the fastest way to get a Russian visa," he murmured back before kissing the top of her head. To the casual passerby, they looked like the picture of wedded bliss.

LaSalle had been true to his word; he had followed Leader's instructions to the letter. They had left the Salt Mine later that afternoon with the information from the FBI investigation, a floor plan of the laboratory, and airline tickets and passports for both sets of aliases. Wilson had also loaded up bullets for Eastern Europe, in case they crossed native supernatural creatures that needed to be put down. Martinez had just enough time to make it home, pack, and meet Wilson at the airport for an overnight flight to Helsinki with a stopover at Charles de Gaulle. Officially, Davis Watson and Tessa Marvel were conducting business in Finland for a week, looking at possible acquisitions for Discretion Minerals. Once they touched down in Helsinki, they emerged as Mr. and Mrs. Williams, eager to move onto the next leg of their honeymoon.

Irkutsk had the distinction of being the capital of the Irkutsk Oblast in Russia and the closest airport to Listvyanka, a tourist destination on the southwestern edge of Lake Baikal. A UNESCO world heritage site, Baikal was an ancient rift lake surrounded by mountains on all sides. Its renown was as massive as its size: the world's oldest, deepest, largest, and clearest freshwater lake. Martinez wouldn't have minded visiting during the summer and getting on the water, but Mr. and Mrs. Williams were fortunate enough to catch the tail end of ice season, with transparency up to one meter deep.

With two overnight flights and over thirty plus hours of travel, they had plenty of time to get caught up on the FBI's investigation and review the lab layout and security checkpoints. They had dedicated their first day to "sightseeing" the city, taking a walking tour that serendipitously passed by the lab and its surroundings. It wasn't far from the university, so there was always a steady stream of people nearby. At various points during their stroll, Wilson had pulled out his compass, but there was no trace of Lukin.

When they had returned to their suite, there was a message tucked under their door to be at a particular restaurant for a late lunch in Listvyanka the next day. This morning, they had taken the train to the self-proclaimed gateway to Baikal. The rail had swayed back and forth along the switchbacks as it climbed up the mountain. They had walked through the village and on the ice, bought treats from local vendors who relied on a steady stream of tourists, and played their part until it came time for their lunch date.

At least the weather is making posing as honeymooners easy, Martinez thought, tapping into Wilson's core heat; even though she was five inches taller than him, the height difference was minimal when they sat. The waiter approached their table bearing their meal.

"Pelmeni for the lady," he spoke in heavily accented English. He lifted the cover from the bowl, and the fragrant steam that rolled out was inviting enough. Martinez couldn't wait to try the bite-sized meat-filled dumplings bobbing in the dark, rich broth. "And for the gentleman, braised beef stroganoff." The waiter placed an extra towel under the dish. "Be careful, the plate is hot."

Martinez peeled herself away from Wilson's warmth and tucked into her dumplings and soup. She stared out at the soaring views from her mountainous perch while the hot broth brought warmth back to her cheeks. She conceded that there were worse ways to wait for their contact.

Wilson gingerly touched his plate and found it warm, but far from hot. He rolled a generous pile of egg noodles in the thick sauce and speared a piece of meat so tender it almost broke apart on the fork. His first bite was delicious, if a little messy, and a dabble of sauce dripped on the side of his mouth. He quickly maneuvered napkins to wipe it off. His slight of hand went unnoticed by all except Martinez, whose close proximity and keen perception allowed her to catch sight of him swiping the extra napkin the waiter had left under the plate into his lap.

"Good?" Martinez asked suggestively.

"Better than good," Wilson replied. He deftly pocketed the plastic package tucked in the folds of the napkin. "Charlotte, how would you feel about heading back to the hotel after lunch?"

"I think that sounds wonderful," she replied with a grin, and popped another dumpling into her mouth. As they ate, an older couple a few tables over smirked knowingly at each other—*ah, amore.*

*****

It took them a little over three hours before they were back at their suite in Irkutsk. Martinez started prattling on about their day at the lake while Wilson swept the room for bugs and checked for signs of interference. It was bordering on a stream of consciousness by the time Wilson gave her the all clear.

Wilson unearthed two access cards from the depths of his inner pocket. They each had a hole punched through the top for fastening to one's clothing. The fronts bore the name of the lab in Cyrillic with its logo on the bottom half; the backs had a magnetic strip. Pressed between them was a slip of paper with a number: B32. Wilson pulled up the map of the lab and found the room; they would have to swipe past two security doors, one of which had a camera. Martinez pulled out a makeup case packed with dozens of compartments, their kit hidden in plain sight—no one questioned the size of a woman's vanity.

They each donned latex gloves, and Wilson wiped down both sides of the plastic cards with alcohol swabs to remove dirt and his fingerprints. Martinez pulled out adhesive sheets of thin clear plastic and two plastic baggies, each of which held their photo, sized for European passports. The close-range electric jammer and cards were all they needed to get through the tech, but if they were to run into someone, having their photos on the cards added extra creditability.

They secured their photos to the cards and laid the sticky clear plastic over the top. Martinez unearthed the razor blade she'd purchased on arrival to cut the excess, leaving a small tab on the corner opposite the magnetic strip for easy removal when they needed to dump the cards, sans their pictures. She pulled out a selection of ID holders, finding something that would fit the cutout.

They agreed that cover of night was best, not only for maneuvering to the lab itself, but there would be fewer people inside. There was some debate on whether to go tonight or tomorrow. Martinez was a proponent for going tonight, in case Forester was being held somewhere else and they needed to regroup.

Wilson argued for tomorrow, for a couple of reasons. First, there would be more city traffic tonight—Saturday night—and a higher chance of being seen. Second, it would be ideal to take out Forester—and if necessary, the lab—the night before their flight out. If they went tonight and found Forester, they would have to make two forays into the lab, which increased their risk of being caught. As to Martinez's concern that Forester was no longer there, if Forester had been moved, it didn't matter if they found out tonight or tomorrow. They were still screwed.

Martinez came around to his point of view, and they spent the next few hours mapping out possible routes to the lab, fallback positions, and meet-ups in case things went pear-shaped tomorrow night. Once night fell, they hid the access cards with their other covert equipment and dressed for a night out.

They bar hopped, making a perimeter around the lab, noting possible entrances and exits, locations of the streetlights, the distribution of foot and car traffic, which paths were more frequented by the locals, the number of windows that remained lit in the lab after hours, and when they went dark. Feigning inebriation wasn't difficult, especially when everyone else on the street was in various states of intoxication as the night wore on. Without entering the lab itself, they had a good handle on the situation they would be embarking on tomorrow.

In the wee hours of the night, Martinez finally got to change into her pajamas and curl up on the soft fur rug in front of the fireplace, body flush with just the right amount of Russian vodka.

Chapter Twenty-Four

Irkutsk, Siberia, Russia
15th of April, 1:00 a.m. (GMT+8)

Dressed in black, Martinez and Wilson slipped out of their hotel through the fire escape that debouched in a dark alley off the main street. It was cold but dry, and most of the snow had melted away. There were still people on the streets, but nothing compared to this time last night. They silently crept along the route they had hammered out at the hotel earlier in the day—it kept to isolated streets with less streetlight coverage, and would bring them to the rear entrance to the lab. Every time they passed under a light, he checked his compass for Lukin, but there was still no sign.

Wilson pulled out his access card while Martinez readied her electric jammer to scramble the camera just inside the door. They held their breath; this was the moment of truth—how reliable was their mole? He swiped the strip, and the red light flipped to green as they heard the audible click of the lock opening. He opened the door and stood back while Martinez swept the immediate seam of the ceiling until she found the camera and focused her jammer's beam.

She motioned to Wilson, and they both stepped inside and

shut the door behind them. The jammer had a range of ten meters, which should get them around the corner and past video surveillance. They forwent their flashlights and followed the hallway, dimly illuminated by every fourth light on half power. They took a right and then the first left after the breakroom, which smelled of reheated leftovers and mugs in need of a good washing. They descended the stairs to the basement and came upon the second locked door, this time without a camera.

Its front was covered with Cyrillic warnings and pictorial icons that transcended language—do not enter, biohazard, danger, possible death. Wilson used his card again—they had agreed to only use one, in case anyone was checking card usage after the fact. If this became a manhunt, they would be looking for a lone assailant, and Martinez and Wilson would be traveling as a pair. The light turned green and the door opened. Wilson pushed on the door with a gloved hand and entered, with Martinez close behind him.

Unlike the other doors, the casing of Room 32's faintly glowed from the light within. Wilson quietly checked the handle—it was unlocked. He nodded to Martinez, and they screwed on their suppressers and secured their weapons— within reach but out of sight. He was packing magical bullets, she mundane. They donned their access cards as badges, Wilson made a final check on his compass, and they entered.

The room beyond was lined with countertops, with piles of surplus supplies. There was a large industrial freezer that stored samples in sub-zero temperatures, most likely with a monitor and alarm should the inside become too warm. It was lit by humming fluorescent rods that cast everything in a pale sickly yellow light. In the far back corner was a cot with a pillow and crumpled blankets, opposite of which was a dull metallic bedpan. The center of the room was divided by three freestanding lab tables. On the first was a sandwich, chips, and an apple that hadn't been touched, while the second held bottles of mineral water in various states of fullness.

Sitting at the farthest table from the door and precariously perched on a stool with his back to them was the thin form of Dr. Forester. The table was covered in paper—some with writing, others blank—and the man hovered over his work like a dragon with his hoard.

"Just put it on the table like usual," he spoke without turning his head.

Chapter Twenty-Five

Irkutsk, Siberia, Russia
15th of April, 1:30 a.m. (GMT+8)

It had been five days since Dr. Forester's arrival, but he had lost track of time despite the clock on the wall. Every so often, a tray of food and more bottles of water were brought it and his bedpan changed, but all other markers of daily routine disappeared from his notice. His eyes sunk further into his gaunt face, not that he could have known—there were no mirrors in the room, and the distorted reflection in the paper towel dispenser didn't give a true picture of his decline. He wouldn't have cared anyway—he had more important things to think about, and he didn't need a timepiece to know he was running out of time. His research was vital, and he needed to get it all down before the cancer took him.

He rued the fact that the lab hadn't sought him out sooner. Here, he could have worked unfettered by rules and regulations, no longer hamstrung by the arbitrary rulings of committees and councils. They appreciated his genius. They would make sure his ideas lived on after him. This was nothing less than his legacy.

Forester feverishly scribbled more formulas and drew more

benzene molecules to show the progression of his experiments. His theories were multi-disciplined—he had so much he needed to include! He was working from memory, as he had destroyed all his notes before leaving Ukraine, but it was all in there, tucked away in his gray and white matter. He just had to retrieve it. They wanted to take his notes daily, but he wouldn't hear of it. You wouldn't present a symphony one bar at a time or serve a dish one ingredient at a time. No, he would need all of it in front of him to write it all down, to make sure the sum was greater than its parts. When he was finished—that's when they would get it, and it would take their breath away.

There were times that the fatigue and nausea stopped his progress, moments where he had to rest on the cot in the corner or eat a little something with the help of his anti-nausea tablets, but it wasn't long before the fire behind his eyes burned bright again. Compelled to explain his process, Forester pressed on.

Somewhere in the back of his mind, he heard the click of the door opening. *It must be time for more food*, he thought to himself while he wrote on. "Just put it on the table like usual," he spoke without turning his head.

Martinez and Wilson entered the room and closed the door behind them. *Think, think, think.* Wilson started welling up his magic. "You asked to see us, Dr. Forester?" he spoke ingratiatingly.

"Did I?" Forester answered without stopping writing. "I can't imagine why. I've been batting you away ever since I got here so I can finish my work in peace and quiet."

"That's why you wanted to speak to us," Wilson pressed. "To update us on your progress. How much have you told us about your work?"

Forester harrumphed, finally looking up from his work. "I told you, you'll see it when it's finished, and not a second sooner."

"Surely, you must have notes or files somewhere else?" Wilson asked.

The doctor guffawed. "And let those morons at the Institute steal my work and take my credit? No way! It's all in here"—he tapped the side of his head—"where it's safe."

"It's too bad that the last batch of salt couldn't be retrieved." Wilson tried to keep his magic smooth and steady, but Forester was unstable and Wilson felt like he wasn't the first one to charm him recently.

Forester shook his head dismissively. "No matter, we can make more once we have the right supplies and equipment."

"So there isn't any more anywhere else?" Wilson inquired, still focused on his magic.

"Who would know how to make it?!" Forester exclaimed, and laughed at his own joke.

Wilson slowly approached, bringing to bear the full force of his will. "Congratulations on finishing your work, Dr. Forester. If you'll hand over the papers, we can start production."

Forester dropped his pen and shook his head. Something

wasn't right. It wasn't the nausea or the wave of fatigue; it wasn't hunger or thirst; he didn't need to void. But his brain screamed out that something was very wrong, and like a frightened animal, he bolted, jumping off his stool, and yelled, "You're trying to steal my work, aren't you?!"

"Calm down, Dr. Forester. You want me to take the papers from you," Wilson informed him, again pumping a full dose of enchantment in his words, surprised by the resistance he was encountering. By now, the poor man should be offering up every paper in the room to Wilson's hand.

"That's ridiculous! This is my work! This is my legacy!" Forester's voice became louder and more ragged with each assertion. His eyes were bloodshot from the sleepless nights and wild with frenzy.

Martinez reached into her pocket and grabbed her rosary. *Hail Mary, full of grace, the Lord is with thee.* "Steve, what about Jane?"

Forester blinked a few times, finding his bearings once again. His eyes were still red, but some of the mania had left them as his posture sank back down. "Janey?"

"You wanted us to bring Janey your papers, so she could understand how important your work is." Martinez let go of the rosary and eased off after the magical thump she'd just hit over Forester's head.

Forester suddenly looked very fragile and very tired. "I didn't want things to turn out like this," he said in a small voice.

"She knows," Martinez reassured him, and infused more magic in her words. "You've worked very hard and now it's time to rest. You've earned your time to rest. Why don't you lie down on the cot?"

It seemed the most logical course of action to Forester—he was very tired and he had worked nonstop since he'd arrived. "Maybe just a short nap."

He moved over to the cot and Martinez met him there. Wilson remained still, not wanting to upset the now-settled Forester. "Let me help you," Martinez replied. She pulled the pillow off the cot and straightened the blanket over him after he reclined.

"All you have to do is relax and go to sleep," Martinez lowered her voice to a soft singsong, streaming a thread of magic so delicate, it was no thicker than spider's silk. "It's going to be all right now. I'm here. I've got you. I won't leave until you are asleep."

Forester closed his eyes and a look of serenity came over the troubled face. Martinez gripped the pillow with both hands and slowly but firmly pressed down, still speaking her magically-laced litany of reassurances. He didn't fight or thrash, and Martinez held fast until there was a final shudder from Forester's frail frame.

Without a word, Wilson moved into action, gathering all the paperwork scattered across the table. He then checked the floors, cabinets, and drawers for any hidden stashes. After a few minutes, Martinez stopped her enchantment and removed the pillow, placing it under Forester's head. She pulled off her thicker gloves and donned thin latex ones before checking for a pulse, just to be certain. At some point, Forester had opened his eyes, but there was nothing in them now. Martinez closed his lids; it was as if he was just sleeping.

Although it seemed longer, Martinez knew it couldn't have been more than a few minutes before Wilson approached them with a pair of short scissors. "We'll need some of his hair to scrub our magic from the scene, in case the Ivory Tower investigates."

Martinez let out a short bitter laugh. "How much karma is that going to cost me? I already killed him with magic."

Wilson caught bits of hair in the baggie before closing it. "You killed him with a pillow. You used magic to make sure he wasn't alone or afraid."

Wilson took a final look over the room to make sure there were no physical traces of their presence. "We should leave. I've got the papers and the hair. Out the same way we came in." Martinez put her thicker gloves back on. "If Chloe and Dot haven't covered it yet, I'll show you how to scrub your signature back at the hotel."

Martinez gave him a nod, and they slipped out the door.

Epilogue

Edmond, Oklahoma, USA
17th of April, 7:30 p.m. (GMT-5)

Jane Kranton nodded as the voice on the other line spoke. Her husband, Mark, could hear the crests and valleys of the tone but none of the words. "I see," Jane finally spoke. "Thank you for calling and letting me know, Agent Martinez." She hung up the phone and answered Mark's entreating stare. "It's the FBI. They think my dad has fled the country. He's outside FBI jurisdiction now, but they'll continue to monitor for any attempts at reentry into the US."

Mark stood up and wrapped his arms around his wife and nestled her head against his chest. He couldn't tell if this was good or bad news, so he waited for Jane to tell him. When she remained still and silent, he tried levity, "At least he won't spontaneously show up at the front door again."

A nervous laugh escaped Jane's lips. "You always look for the silver lining." She wrapped her arms around his waist. "When he came here, I didn't even give him a chance to tell me he had cancer. He had to call me from a jail cell before I would listen."

Mark was a gentle man, but he firmly put his foot down. "You are not the bad guy in this story. He escaped custody and fled the country under suspicion of bioterrorism. Not giving him a chance isn't even in the same ballpark."

Maddy's heavy footfalls on the stairs gave them adequate warning. Jane smiled when their daughter rounded the corner into the kitchen. "Why aren't you in bed, missy?" Jane asked in a firm voice.

"Mommy, there's a monster under my bed," she whined.

"There is? Well, you know the drill," Jane replied. She opened the cabinet under the sink and produced a heavy mag light—Mark insisted on stocking the house with those, as they could also double as a weapon in a pinch. Jane offered her hand to her daughter, and Maddy gladly slipped her small hand inside. Mark heard the pair ascend the stairs and his wife's voice ask, "You know what we do to monsters?"

"Bang them over the head!" Maddy chanted back.

Those are my girls, Mark crowed to himself as he returned to the sink of dishes.

THE END

The agents of The Salt Mine will return in *Ground Rules*

Printed in Great Britain
by Amazon